The Mahjong Maramas

GW00374425

by Jamie J

with special thanks to:

Abi Nickell: Advisor (USA)
Kirsty Pearce: Advisor (UK)
Julie Peeks: Advisor and Editor (Fiji)
Vivian Tang: Advisor and Editor (Hong Kong)
Leanne Pounder: Advisor and Cover Designer (USA)
Christopher Nickell: Website Designer
https://jamiejlaine.com/(USA)
Queenie Thompson: Founder of the Fijian Mahjong Maramas (Fiji)
Juana Lovell: Creator of the Mahjong Maramas Name (Australia)

and all who volunteered to read,
review and give valuable advice along the way:

Janise Allyn-Smith (Maryland, USA) Malcolm Fialho (Fiji),
Peter Hendicott (Australia), Diana Lewis (Fiji),
Roger Nibler (USA), Janet O'Toole (UK), Helen Sykes (Fiji),
David Tatman (USA), Catherine Tatman (Hawaii, USA)
and Joon Sim Toh (Kuala Lumpur, Malaysia)

This story is a work of fiction. All characters, events and incidents and most name places, spring from the imagination of the authors. Any resemblance to real events is entirely coincidental.

No part of this book may be reproduced in any form, stored in a retrieval system, or transmitted by any means, electronic, mechanical, photocopying recording or otherwise without written permission from the authors, except for the use of brief quotations in book reviews.

Copyright © 2021, James & Elaine Pounder
All rights reserved

Table of Contents

Chapter 1

The Game

"Chow!"

"No, you can't chow from the right," said Sui Ling. "You can only chow from the left."

"Oh, it confuses me when we change from playing the Western game to the Chinese and back again."

"Cathy, concentrate. Remember, you can only chow from the left in both versions."

Penny chipped in, "Girls, girls, come on now. I think it's time to take a break. Actually, it's about time for a glass of wine."

"Oh, I agree," said Stella, "I love wine-o-clock. What did you bring from your wine cellar to delight our palates today, Penny?"

"Beaujolais Nouveau, of course because it's November. Gregory picked up a dozen bottles on Thursday and I managed to snaffle two for us."

The Mahjong ladies couldn't be further from China, where the game originated, if they tried. Ruth's home, where they were just about to taste this year's offering of the famous Beaujolais Nouveau, was a listed 17th century thatched cottage in the picturesque village of Hazelby in the heart of Yorkshire, the largest county in England. This historic county sits almost two hundred miles north of London in the north-central part of England between the Pennines and the North Sea. and is famously known as God's Own County, no doubt nicknamed as such by a Yorkshireman.

Ruth headed to the kitchen and returned with five wine glasses along with some nibbles. It wouldn't do for them to get drunk in the middle of the day, she thought. Ruth never forgot the day Stella had one too many glasses and not enough to eat and ended up stumbling into George as she left the house rather late one afternoon. Ruth smiled wryly to herself as she recalled how George, in typical fashion, didn't say a word, but looked at her with eyes that could convey his every thought and which she had learned to read only too well.

It was hardly surprising that he didn't drink after having been raised by a father who was rarely sober. In fact, it was probably because of George's steady, sober character that he had become one of the U.K.'s most respected Chief Constables with many professional accolades to his name. Ruth's thoughts amused her as she reflected on the fact that she had spent a lifetime with non-drinking men because her late father had been a Methodist Minister who didn't drink either. Like her mother, Ruth had no such convictions. She was partial to both wine and spirits and could certainly let her hair down and party with the best of them, but always under control, of course.

"Cheers everyone!" Penny's toast was met with cheers from all as they clinked their glasses in their toast to the new wine, anticipating its sweet simple taste.

"Mmmm that's one fine wine, Penny."

"Thanks, Cathy, I must say I have to agree," Penny said with a smile.

By now Ruth was handing around the nibbles and cake, chipping in with, "I agree too; I think it's even better than last year's and that was good!"

"Here Stella," offered Ruth, "have a piece of this gluten free lemon cake I baked with you in mind, after all, you really didn't eat much at lunch today."

"Oh, no, I couldn't possibly eat cake. I put on three pounds over the long weekend; so disappointing after only losing two at fat club last week!"

"Oh, tell me about it," said Cathy. "I only have to look at a piece of cake to put on weight so I've decided I might as well eat it anyway."

Ruth laughingly passed Cathy a slice too.

"What about you Sui Ling; would you like a piece?"

"Just a tiny piece, please."

Cathy, in her usual forthright manner, did not surprise anyone when she said, "The only one who can afford to eat cake and all she wants is a tiny piece!"

Stella chirped up, "That's precisely why Sui Ling has

never had a weight problem. Perhaps we should all follow her lead."

"I wish I could. I'd love to be that thin," said Cathy.

Ruth was quick to say, "You mean slim, Cathy, slim, not thin."

"Come on, Stella, you have to eat when you drink. We don't want another one of those George incidents now, do we? It took me a while to convince him that we're serious players and not a just a set of winos using mahjong as a cover when he came home early that day and found you stumbling out of the door!"

"Okay, just a small piece and then let's play another game."

Very soon, Ruth, Sui Ling, Penny and Stella were shuffling the tiles and making that clickety-clack sound known as 'twittering of the sparrows' which signalled it was time to stop talking and focus.

Cathy, the newest member of this little group, picked up her notebook as it was her turn to sit out and watch, and she had decided to start making notes to help her remember the rules of what was, to her, still a very confusing game.

"Who is East Wind?" she asked.

"You are, Penny," said Sui Ling, "Ruth didn't win the last round so it moves to you. Look, let me give you a little recap now that you've decided to keep a notebook. Once you have all of your tiles, your aim is to build them into sets by keeping any tiles you pick up from the wall that are useful and discarding those that are of no help to you. Remember a Pung is a set of three identical tiles and a Kong a set of four while a Chow is a run of three tiles in the same suit. Now, you can achieve Mahjong by collecting four Pungs, Kongs or Chows and a matching pair or by collecting all the tiles you need for one of the special hands. There are too many special hands for me to run through, but you can use my book as a guide as we play. In fact, you can keep it so that you can study the hands at home and I'll order another copy for myself. I'm sure you will still have questions, so do ask them when you need to as that's how you'll learn."

"Thank you. That's so kind of you," said Cathy appreciatively.

They all then started to build their walls with a reminder from Sui Ling that they only needed them to be seventeen tiles long for the Chinese game. As soon as the walls were built, Penny threw the dice.

"Eleven."

Sui Ling, sitting opposite Penny, immediately knew it was her turn to break the wall, so she took the first four tiles. One by one they each took sets of four tiles until they all had twelve, and then Penny took the first and third from the top layer of the wall with everyone else taking one more tile each and then they were ready to play.

Just before play began, Sui Ling, reminded everyone, "Don't forget we need to finish with a pair of twos, fives or eights in hand, girls."

Penny discarded her first tile and down they came in quick succession: Red Dragon, West Wind, Nine Bamboo, White Dragon, One Character, West Wind and Seven Circles at which point Stella quickly claimed that tile.

"Pung!"

Stella was not only quick off the mark to call but also quick to pick up Sui Ling's discarded Seven Circles. She then went on to throw out a Green Dragon and play continued.

Round and round they went with occasional Pungs and Chows being called and even one Kong before Ruth picked up a tile and said, "I'm fishing".

Play continued cautiously, everyone knowing that now was not a good time to be throwing out a 2, a 5 or an 8, but it was immaterial because in Ruth's very next turn, she picked the very tile she needed from the wall and shouted "Mahjong!" with glee.

"Okay, Cathy, you can take my place now and I'll sit out," offered Sui Ling.

Penny, however, was quick to say, "I think we should have another glass of Beaujolais before we play the next round."

"Great idea!" said Stella, and Ruth then busied herself pouring glasses of wine as everyone else made themselves comfortable on the sofas. While waiting for Ruth to return, Penny asked Cathy what they all knew to be a bit of a sensitive question, for almost as soon as she'd joined their Mahjong group, she'd told them that she and Dan had been trying to have a baby for three years already.

"How was your romantic evening-in, Cathy?"

"Oh, don't talk to me about romance. There's not much romance involved with a thermometer in hand that has you running to the bedroom at the dictate of a temperature chart! Actually, we ended up watching Netflix and getting hooked on the series that you recommended, you know, 'Breaking Bad'. We watched three episodes and didn't want to stop, but Dan said if he didn't get to sleep then, he'd be like 'death warmed up' on site the next day!"

"Oh, I know, Gregory and I were the same as we watched at least an episode every night and several during the weekends until we'd watched all five seasons." said Penny. "To tell you the truth, I saw so many parallels between Walter and Gregory, it made me laugh, well at least until Walter's character became dark. I'm not sure that Gregory would take that as a compliment though so best not mention it to him when you see him at the Golf Club Christmas Ball."

"I loved that series, too, and was sad when it ended, but now I'm into 'The Great British Bake Off'," interjected Stella. "I missed it when it aired, but I'm watching the series from the beginning. Peter's not too thrilled about my addiction though because I keep trying out my creations on him. You know what he's like."

"Oh, I can just imagine him saying, 'Stella, how on earth can I keep in good shape when you keep serving up sugary rubbish!'"

Everyone laughed at Penny's mimicry, even Stella, as Penny had Peter's plum-throated accent down to a T.

"YK is like that too. He rarely eats anything but fruit after dinner. In fact, that's all most Chinese families have for dessert, except at Chinese New Year of course, when it's all sugar on sugar."

"Oh girls, I must tell you about the programmes George and I have been watching on YouTube," said Ruth. "They focus on cold cases that are solved, sometimes after decades. They are really fascinating. Advances in DNA profiling have helped in a lot of cases, but sometimes they're solved by someone just refusing to let them go cold and persistently pushing and probing until they find the answers."

"Oh, I saw something like that on Netflix," Sui Ling was quick to say. "I think it was called 'Unsolved Mysteries', but, of course, they focused on cases that still remain unsolved and that frustrated me, so goodness knows how the families involved cope."

"Funny you should raise that, Sui Ling," said Ruth. "Do you know that there was a murder just ten miles from here in Bentham Woods that was never solved?"

"Oh, yes, I do recall something in the news about it, but I don't know the details. What happened?"

"Well, it was about twenty years ago. George told me a bit about it, but he wasn't involved, of course, because it happened during the time he was seconded as an advisor to the Hong Kong police force. A young woman, whose name I can't remember, but who I believe was from Leeds, was found dead in the undergrowth by a couple walking their dog one morning."

Stella joined the conversation, "Oh, I remember that case, most everyone in the village and several others were questioned. At one point, they focused on all the men who owned Range Rovers. I remember this because they came and questioned Peter too."

"That's awful," said Cathy. "I'd hate it if Dan was a suspect in a police investigation. I'm glad we didn't live here then."

"He wasn't a suspect, Cathy! It was just the police making routine enquiries and those who owned Range Rovers got a second visit after the team investigating her murder suggested the vehicle involved might be a Range Rover. As you know, Range Rovers are ten-a-penny in the countryside, so most everyone got a second visit. As I recall, they didn't find anyone with a connection to the girl up here, and before long the investigation seemed to focus on people she knew in Leeds where she came from."

"Did you live here at the time Penny?" enquired Sui Ling.

"Yes, but we were quite new to the area as Gregory had just started his residency in York, and I was busy setting up home. Besides, the police never even came to our place, probably because we didn't own a Range Rover and our little Ford obviously didn't interest them! That's probably why I don't recall the details."

"Well," said Sui Ling, we were living in Scotland at the time and setting up a new restaurant in Edinburgh, which is probably why I don't know the details either. We had managers in at the Green Dragon down here at the time and they never really mentioned the case. In fact, by the time we returned after almost two years away, it was no longer a topic of conversation. I didn't even know it hadn't been solved. I do love a good murder mystery though. In fact, I like solving puzzles, full stop! I've actually been reading some Miss Marple books and watching episodes of 'Rosemary & Thyme' but they're just fictional, of course. I wonder what it would be like to get involved in a real case. What do you think Ruth? Does the Force need a little enthusiastic team to pick up where they left off in Bentham Woods?"

"Hahaha, I don't think they need a bunch of interfering busybodies getting involved. Besides, what experience do any of us have in solving crimes?"

"Maybe, we haven't, but one thing we do have is time and we all love trying to outwit each other with strategy around the Mahjong table," added Penny. "I think it would be exciting trying to work out who did it, and a huge help if we can solve the mystery. After all, the murderer may still be out there somewhere and, so far, has certainly managed to avoid capture."

"I think that sounds awfully dangerous, Penny, and I'm not sure that Dan would approve of me getting involved in anything like that," said Cathy. "What do you think, Stella?"

"I'm not sure I want to get involved and I don't think I have anything to offer anyway. I was a secretary before marrying Peter and all I can find my way around is a keyboard."

"Don't sell yourself short Stella," said Penny. "You did work in a legal firm before you married Peter, so you've got some idea about how the legal system works at least, and you could keep us on the straight and narrow, legally speaking."

"Yes, but there's a big difference between what happens after someone is caught and the legal team go to work and what is actually involved in catching someone."

"Be that as it may, you have some knowledge and besides, we don't all need to have a full set of skills. We can all bring something of value to the table," responded Penny," and Ruth, you've been married to George for almost thirty years so must have gathered some insight on how to go about solving crimes."

"Oh, that reminds me, I've got our 30th wedding anniversary invitations for you all. George picked them up from the printer at the weekend. I'm really looking forward to being able to renew our vows at the chapel where my dad married us thirty years ago though I'm sad he's no longer with us. He would have loved to have witnessed it. Still, mum will be here because my brother, Matthew, and his wife, Judy, will collect her from the nursing home on their way over."

Stella chipped in, "Oh, Peter and I had dinner over at the Golf Club last week and the new chef is something else; his food is out of this world, so I don't think you're going to be disappointed holding your reception there."

"Oh, that's great news," Ruth responded. "Now let me get the invitations for you before I forget."

"Thanks Ruth, now let's get back to Sui Ling's idea of us turning into crime busters," suggested Penny. "I'm all for it and with the boys away at boarding school I've got more time on my hands than I know what to do with. Besides, I just love the idea of becoming a super sleuth! Come on girls, let's at least consider it. After all, if that young girl had been one of our daughters, none of us would have liked the case to just lie dormant and be effectively forgotten."

"I'm definitely in, Penny," replied Sui Ling. "I've already told you that unsolved murders frustrate me. I love puzzles, and I really get satisfaction from seeing problems solved."

"Okay, here they are, girls," said Ruth, who had returned and was handing the invitations around.

"Oh, they're gorgeous," said Stella. "I love the hand-painted flowers. I'm guessing you created them yourself."

"You know me too well, Stella. I enjoyed every minute of creating them. Now, what did I miss when I went upstairs to fetch the invitations?"

"Sui Ling and I have just been confirming that we're up

for a little investigation," responded Penny. "But you still need to answer my point about having been married to George for almost thirty years, meaning you must have gathered some insight on how to go about solving crimes."

"Well, I guess I do have some knowledge about crime fighting after being with George for so long, not that he shares everything with me because some of his information is quite confidential. However, he does sometimes bounce ideas off me as he puzzles over challenging cases and needs someone outside of the team to give a fresh perspective. In all honesty though, I really don't know enough about this particular case or where to start because George was never involved in it in the first place. In fact, by the time we came back from Hong Kong, the case was effectively shelved pending new information or evidence, and I can't remember anything ever coming forward."

"Okay, so I'm going to take that to mean you're in and can be tasked with getting all the information you can from George."

"Whoa, Penny, I didn't say I was in, but all right, I'll talk to George about the case to find out what he knows or can find out for us."

"Stella you already know you have something to offer and, Cathy, you come from Leeds so you have something in common with the victim. Do at least think about it. We'll be like private detectives pondering on all that has been discovered so far and sifting through what is known to find the missing key. In fact, we can have our own file with everything we know mapped out so that we can find the links that have obviously been missed. Who knows, we might just end up as heroes of the day and more importantly, get justice for the girl and her family."

"I'll think about it, Penny, just don't push me as I need to process the idea before I can commit."

"Okay, Stella. What about you Cathy?"

"If it's just a table-top investigation and we don't have to go out as undercover investigators, then yes, and you're right, I do have Leeds in common with the girl even though I moved to Sheffield when I was sixteen."

"Then we're all set or at least thinking about it," said Penny with an air of excitement. "Let's talk about it again next time we meet."

"All right, girls, it's coming up to two forty-five, so do we want another game or shall we call it a day?"

"I have to leave now Ruth," said Stella, "because I need to pick up Peter's suits from the dry cleaners in Harrogate. He's off to chambers again in Leeds tomorrow and will be away for the whole week because he has a new case starting on Monday."

Sui Ling agreed, "YK and I have a family dinner tonight to celebrate his sister-in-law, Margie's, birthday so I'd best be on my way too."

"Me too," said Cathy. "I must get back as this is my most fertile time of the month, and I need to prep dinner to

14

feed Dan up so he has the energy for another attempt at baby making if the signs say it's time to strike!"

The girls laughed and said farewell to each other with a plan to meet up at Stella's for their next game.

Chapter 2

The Birth of Sleuths

The first chime of the doorbell rang out at nine-thirty a.m. exactly, and Stella headed to the door to find Ruth and Sui Ling shaking their umbrellas under the rather grand portico.

"Come in, come in quickly. The rain has warmed the temperature up a little, but I really don't know whether I prefer the freezing cold or the cold rain!"

No sooner had she escorted them into the lounge than the doorbell rang again, and this time she found Penny and Cathy eager to enter and escape from the driving rain.

Everyone gathered around the huge open fireplace that had been keeping Peter's family warm for generations in Hazelby Manor. His family had owned the Manor since it and the land for miles around were bequeathed to one of his ancestors back in the days of William the Conqueror.

Stella offered hot chocolate all round to help them thaw.

"Mmm, that's divine," said Penny. "I'm going to ignore the fact that it's loaded with cream and I'll just do extra laps in the pool to work the calories off!"

"Oh, you'll be fine; just enjoy it," Stella replied. Of course, Stella never prioritised exercise over the opportunity to indulge the palate.

They all sat around drinking their hot chocolates and the topic of the murder quickly raised its head as Sui Ling remarked on how she'd not managed to get the conversation they'd had last week out of her head.

"Did you talk to George, Ruth?" she asked.

"I did, but he was not very forthcoming because he doesn't approve of us getting involved and said that it was a matter for the police and not for a group of would-be sleuths. In actual fact, he told me that because we weren't around at the time, he knows very little about the case. To be honest girls, I think we're hitting a brick wall with George."

"Okay, if that's the case," said Penny, "we need to start digging ourselves. Let's all make some time this week to find out what we can about the case and we can bring it all to the table next week. Agreed, girls?"

Sui Ling responded with a resounding 'yes' for when anything bothered her, she needed to get to the bottom of it as quickly as possible. Ruth nodded in agreement and Cathy and Stella also agreed, although somewhat less enthusiastically.

"Okay, with that settled, anyone for an extra cup of hot chocolate before we start to play?"

"I'll have one please, Stella," said Ruth. "By the way, how was Margie's birthday dinner Sui Ling?"

"Oh, it was lovely, Ruth. Edwin had organised everything down to the tiniest detail. The two of them are still such lovebirds after all these years. I wish YK was a little more like his brother, but romance has never been his forte. Still, he's a good man in his own way, so I'm not really complaining.

"Actually, we had a bit of a drama the next day as we had a call from our son, Michael, to say that our three-year-old grandson, Harry, had been rushed to a hospital in Shenzhen with suspected meningitis. We were extremely concerned until we got his next call about six hours later to say that it was a false alarm, thank goodness! They kept him in overnight for observation, but by the next morning, he was as perky as ever and allowed home."

"Oh, so typical of children, up one minute and down the next," said Stella.

"I know, but all the same, I do find it terribly hard with them being so far away. I'll be glad when the bridge he's working on is finished and they can come home. The trouble is, there's no knowing where his next contract could take him. I think it's just par for the course for engineers to travel around the world on projects these days and to be honest, I think Michael quite likes that aspect, though I have to be honest and say, we don't! In fact, I don't think YK will ever get over his disappointment that Michael didn't follow in his footsteps as he really wanted him to take over running the Green Dragon Group, but I knew that was never going to happen. Michael was an engineer at heart from the time he could toddle; his toys were always being dismantled and rebuilt. Besides, he would never have met Xiu Ying if he'd remained in Yorkshire, and they seem really happy together. She's also a very good mum to Harry."

18

"Does Harry have a Chinese name too?" asked Cathy.

"He does; it's Li Wei, but only Xiu Ying's parents and grandparents use his Chinese name. Even Xiu Ying prefers to call him Harry, but then again, she studied in Australia, so is as Westernised as Michael. Saying that, she never chose to have a Western name herself, for she just loves her Chinese name and so does Michael because it means beautiful flower. Besides, Xiu Ying is easy for Westerners to pronounce and often Western names are adopted just to make it easier for others."

Stella joined the conversation by saying, "I remember meeting your daughter-in-law when they came to see you with Harry, who was no more than a few months old at the time. What a pretty girl Xiu Ying is and her name certainly suits her and my, you would never have imagined she'd had a baby just months earlier."

Stella had them all laughing when she said, "It always amazes me how quickly some people lose their baby weight, especially Asian women. I'm still trying to lose mine after twenty-seven years!"

"Right girls, let's get the show on the road. I've put the table up in the conservatory where it's lovely and warm despite the cold outside. I thought we'd start with the Chinese game to warm our brains up a little before we switch to the Western version and we really have to start thinking. Besides, it means we can fit more games in. You four can start and I'll clear the cups away and come in to replace whoever is East Wind when it changes."

Two hours later with seven games behind them, Cathy,

who seemed to be getting a little frustrated with not having won a single game, asked if they could stop for lunch soon. They all agreed it was time for a break and everyone pitched in to help Stella, who had prepared a gluten-free vegetarian lasagna and salad, but she did include a lovely garlic baguette for everyone else, not that she wasn't partial to indulging in such treats when the fancy took her.

"Oh, before I forget, Ruth, Gregory and I can confirm that we'll be coming to your 30th wedding anniversary celebration on the 8th of January."

"That's great, Penny." One by one the girls all confirmed that they, too, would be there.

"Have you planned what you're going to be wearing, Ruth?" asked Cathy.

"I would love to be able to wear my original wedding gown, but I'm afraid I've put on far too much weight to be able to do that, so I'm going to buy something new. There are lots of nice outfits in the shops already for Christmas, so I'm sure I'll find an outfit I like."

"Ooh, talking of Christmas," said Penny, "I bought my gown for the Golf Club Christmas Ball last week from that little boutique near the Castle Museum in York. It really is full of wonderfully unique pieces and not too expensive, all things considered."

Cathy quickly added, "Oh, Penny, I've got to find something nice to wear; I've never been to a Ball before."

"Then you're in for a treat. You'll have a great time because Hazelby's Golf Club is renowned for its fun as well as for its fundraising."

"I've still to buy something too," said Stella. "I've been dieting for what seems like an eternity. I really did want to lose at least ten pounds before buying a dress, but time is running out now and there's going to be one Christmas event after another centering around food once December hits next week, so I guess I'm not going to lose even ten ounces let alone ten pounds!"

"What about you, Sui Ling," asked Ruth. "Are you going to wear one of your gorgeous cheongsams?"

"I am, but I've not decided which one yet. I brought so many back from China with me last year that I certainly don't need to have a new one made."

As they neared the end of lunch, Cathy, admiring the beautiful dining room, asked Stella how long she'd lived in the house.

"I've been here since the day I married Peter twenty-nine years ago. Of course, this is your first visit here, isn't it? Would you like to take a look around? It is a rather grand house and I do enjoy showing friends around."

"Oh, that would be lovely, Stella. I've never been in such a grand home; other than visiting places like Chatsworth House."

"Oh, my goodness, we're not on that scale at all, but Hazelby Manor is quite a landmark in this part of the world and though Peter doesn't adhere to the old traditions so much, he's actually Lord of the Manor, Lord Hazelby, if truth be told."

Ruth, Penny and Sui Ling said they'd clear the dishes and get ready for the next game while Stella took Cathy around the house.

"Okay, Cathy, come on, let's start at the top and work our way down."

Stella took Cathy up to the attic where there was a nursery and two single bedrooms, which in their time, had been used by a nursemaid and a lady's maid. From the windows, Cathy got a bird's eye view of the estate which not only featured a large barn, stables and a wooded area, but also a small lake.

"Oh, Stella, the view is out of this world. Do you own all that we can see?"

"Yes, well, I should say, Peter does and it will eventually be passed on to Marcus, of course."

On the first floor, Cathy oohed and aahed as Stella took her from one grand bedroom to the next until she'd seen all seven, four of which had their own en-suites. In addition to the en-suites there was also one large bathroom which featured the original bathtub with quaint legs, but the bathroom had been re-modelled to a standard far beyond what it might have been in days gone by.

From there, Stella took Cathy down to the basement, which featured a large dining kitchen. She told Cathy it had once been a bustling meeting place for staff. She then went on to show her the staff quarters which comprised three small bedrooms to sleep two and a single room for the housekeeper. Finally, they moved on to what had once been an office for the butler and then beyond this to his private quarters and quite an impressive wine cellar.

"It reminds me of Downton Abbey," said Cathy.

Stella laughed. "Oh, I loved watching that programme too, but this place was never in that league. Still, it was quite a hive of activity in its day when Peter's grandparents ruled the roost. Even his parents did a lot of entertaining, but Peter and I are quite low key. In fact, we only have four people to help us. There's Eric and his wife, Brenda, who live in a cottage on the estate and who have been with the family for almost fifty years. Then there's Diane Staunton who comes in from the village to clean four days a week and we also employ her son, Johnny, to help Eric who still likes to care for the grounds despite him not being too well these days."

"Oh, I know Diane, she's in the Monday night water aerobics class that I go to. She's lovely."

"Yes, she is and she's very reliable. I feel comfortable with her and trust is important to me. Okay, let me take you back upstairs and show you the rest of the ground floor." Once back upstairs to the floor on which they'd started, Stella took Cathy into a large reception room, where guests arriving for a function would be welcomed, but which she said was only used very occasionally these days.

From there, they went into the formal dining room with a table that could seat eighteen people and again, Stella explained that this room was seldom used as most of their entertaining today was far less formal and conducted in the part of the house that they considered more homely and inviting and where they spent most of their time.

The two of them then headed back into the conservatory, where, just before sitting down, Cathy spotted a framed wedding photograph of a handsome young couple on the windowsill.

"Oh, Stella, is that you and Peter?"

"It certainly is, but neither of us look quite like that anymore!"

"Wow, what a gorgeous necklace! Was that your 'something blue'?"

"I guess it was, the sapphire was the brightest of blues and the tiny diamonds surrounding it just sparkled in contrast. It was an heirloom that had been in Peter's family for years."

At this, Ruth chipped in, "Oh, I remember your wedding day. It was the first wedding we went to after ours. Whatever happened to that necklace? I haven't seen you wearing it for years?"

"I wish I knew; it went missing a long time ago. I'm still sad about losing it, not only because it was a family heirloom, but because I loved wearing it too."

"Oh, yes that is sad," said Penny. "It's a gorgeous piece of jewellery and must have been quite valuable. Was it stolen?"

"We didn't think so at the time because there was no sign of a break in. Peter said it had probably been misplaced and would surely turn up, but it never did. Such a shame.

Okay, girls," continued Stella, "back to our game; we've got less than two hours of play time left. Cathy, it's your turn to sit out now and if you sit by Ruth, you can watch her strategise with her tiles as she's the master when it comes to the Western game."

One by one they built their walls, but because the flower tiles were included in the Western game, Ruth reminded them that the walls should be eighteen tiles long instead of seventeen.

"Close your wall, Stella," said Sui Ling. "Don't let the spirits in!"

At that, Stella promptly made sure that her wall was touching Sui Ling's on the left and Ruth's on the right to adhere to Mahjong custom and practice.

Play began with Penny as East Wind because she'd rolled the highest number with the dice. After Penny rolled one more time, Ruth, sitting across from her, knew from the roll of the dice that she was designated to break the wall so she did just that and quickly distributed the tiles. "Has anyone got any flowers," asked Ruth, "because I've got two?"

As East Wind gets to take tiles from the flower wall first, Penny quickly took one tile to replace the flower she was holding. Sui Ling passed as she hadn't got any flowers, but Stella took one and finally Ruth was able to take the two tiles she needed from the flower wall and then play started.

Penny discarded the first tile saying, "Six Bamboo."

"Chow," said Ruth and they were off. Tiles were picked up, dropped, punged, konged and chowed for the next thirty minutes before Sui Ling said she was fishing. Sadly, there was no satisfaction for her because the last tile in play was of no use to her, or anyone else. The first game ended without a winner, so a goulash game had to follow.

"Now, this is interesting, Cathy," said Ruth, "This is the first time we've needed to play a goulash game, since you joined us. Watch carefully because before we start to play the next game, we all get to change tiles with each other."

Once the four walls were rebuilt and everyone had their tiles, Penny swapped three with Stella, who was sitting opposite, and Sui Ling swapped three with Ruth. Then they each swapped three tiles with the players on their right and left. Play then commenced as normal with Penny, as East Wind, discarding the first tile.

"Oh, that looks so complicated," said Cathy.

"Don't worry, it will all make sense in time," said Ruth. At two-thirty p.m., they decided to call it a day and have a last cup of tea before saying their farewells and arranging their next meeting at Penny's home in Little Hazelby.

This little hamlet dated back almost three hundred and fifty years according to church records and, as it was only two miles from the border of Hazelby, it was pretty much an extension of the original village.

Penny made sure that none of them would forget they had work to do this week as she reminded them just before they parted that this would be their first week as detectives.

Chapter 3

The Ladies at Home

"Ruth, I can't help! I've already told you that. Why do you want to get involved anyway? This is a matter for the police not some would-be sleuths who have read too much Agatha Christie!"

"But what harm can we do, George? Besides, according to what you've told me, the police have all but given up on the case, yet there's still a family out there hurting and without closure."

"It's not so much the harm that you can do, but the danger you can find yourself in if the killer is still out there. The murderer is not going to be thrilled with any of you if it's revealed you're behind the net closing in."

"George, now you know that's not a good enough reason not to get involved. Imagine if we'd lost a daughter in such circumstances. We'd never want the case to go cold and the files to be effectively shelved. Besides, we've no intention of taking any unnecessary risks. We're just going to go through all that is already known and do some further investigating down paths that seem worthy of investigation. Who knows, we might make some connections or find clues that were missed in the original investigation. Please, George, help us as much as you can. I'm not asking you to compromise your position by telling us anything that is considered best kept undisclosed. I just want you to give us information about what was uncovered and made known when the case was active."

"Okay, Okay, I'll see what I can do, but you must promise me not go anywhere or do anything that would put any of you at risk. I want you to tell me where you are and what you're doing at all times because you could quickly find yourselves in above your heads. Now, I'm hungry, how about we change the subject and have dinner?"

"I bought your favourite T-bone steaks from the butcher today and I've already made a lovely salad to go with them."

"So, you mean you're putting me on a diet again! You know how much I love mashed potatoes and your mushroom sauce when we have steak."

"It's not exactly a diet, George, but we've got so many events coming up in December, I just thought we could both do with getting a head start so we don't look like a couple of porkers come January."

They set the table together, laughing at the vision Ruth's comment had created in their minds as they did so.

"How was work? Did anything interesting happen today?"

"No, just routine stuff, but I did get a call from John. He wanted to talk about a job that he's thinking of applying for. He really wants a move and there's a CID role that has come up which appeals to him. Oh, and he said he wants to come over with Becky this Sunday for lunch. I told him you'd give Becky a call to talk details."

"Oh, how exciting. I wonder if they've got some news to tell us too!"

"Now, now, Ruth, don't get carried away with the possibility of them announcing we're going to become grandparents. They may just want to talk over the idea of this job in the CID."

"I'm not, I'm just letting the idea float through my head because one day it's going to happen. They've been married for four years already."

Again, they found themselves laughing at their shared knowledge that Ruth was more than a little eager to become a grandma.

Both Ruth and George felt comfortable and happy in the solid relationship they had built over the years. They would see quite a lot of their eldest son, John, and his wife, Becky, as their home was less than an hour away, but they seriously missed seeing their youngest son, Tom, who was serving with the British Army in the Middle East. It had been almost a year now since his last visit and they really couldn't wait for him to get back.

After dinner, they cleared up together and then Ruth suggested they watch another age-old mystery being solved on YouTube, but George was in no mood for more cold case discussions and suggested they find a movie to watch instead. Together they settled on the sofa in front of a roaring fire in their beautiful period cottage in Hazelby to watch one of their favourite films, 'Groundhog Day', for at least the fourth time!

Still in Hazelby, but on the eastern outskirts of the village, the television was playing in a large house on a new, exclusive development of just five individually designed properties. However, their television was getting little attention as Cathy and Dan were in the middle of what looked likely to become a full-blown argument over Cathy's involvement with the Mahjong ladies proposed venture.

"No! I will not have a wife of mine getting into who knows what by acting as a detective with not an ounce of training in detective work. It's a hare-brained scheme and probably dangerous. For goodness sake, Cathy, are you bonkers!?"

"No, but I do think the ladies have a point and though I'm not driving this or even particularly eager, I can't see the harm in our doing a little investigation of our own. Who knows, maybe we'll uncover something."

"Seriously, you can't see the harm! I can't believe I'm hearing you say that. There's a murderer on the loose somewhere and you think he's not going to take any action when he discovers that a group of housewives pretending to be detectives could actually uncover him? Whoever he is, he's avoided capture for twenty years, and if you ever get close to revealing his identity, don't you think he might just want to come after you? He's killed once remember; what makes you think he wouldn't do it again, to save his own neck?"

"What do you take me for, a complete idiot? I've no intention of taking unnecessary risks. In fact, I wasn't even that keen on this, but your patronising attitude makes me want to do it. Also, for your information, the killer could just as easily be a woman."

"Look, Cathy, we're supposed to be trying for a baby and I don't want this to interfere. The stress could affect your hormones and I certainly wouldn't want a pregnant wife getting involved in such stupidity. In fact, I refuse to let you do this!"

"You refuse to let me do this! Who do you think you are that you can tell me what I can and can't do! I'm going to do this whether you like it or not!"

"Well, I've no intention of giving you the go ahead. In fact, I don't even want to spend another minute in your company tonight, I'm going to the pub and I'll eat down there too."

As Cathy heard the door slam, her resolve to go ahead with the plan was fired up and her anger at Dan's attempt to control her, not for the first time, reinforced her resolve. She couldn't be bothered making dinner for one, so she made herself a couple of slices of cheese on toast and went into the lounge where the television was still blasting out. She changed the channel just in time to catch the start of 'Emmerdale', her favourite soap.

Half an hour later as the credits were going up, she went back into the kitchen to find something else to eat and soon found just what she fancied, ice-cream. In fact, she took the whole tub back into the lounge with her and started eating her way through it as she flicked through channel after channel before finding 'Ocean's 8', a movie that she'd missed when it was showing in the cinema.

Two hours later she went back into the kitchen, this time with an empty ice-cream tub. There was no sign of Dan and she began to miss him, but she was adamant not to give in to his demands and so chose not to message him. Instead, she switched off the television and lights and went to bed. Sleep eluded her though and around midnight, she heard his key in the door, but as always after a row and a night on the beer, Dan headed straight to the spare room to sleep.

Sui Ling's discussion with her husband that evening was far more positive. She was stir-frying chicken and vegetables when YK came downstairs from his home office around eight p.m. The aroma of garlic and ginger had tempted this workaholic away from his desk and into the kitchen.

"Mmm that smells good. I didn't realise how hungry I was. I've been working solidly since I left the restaurant at two o'clock."

"Oh, why were you over there?"

"David asked me if I could meet him to discuss a few problems. He's got more on his plate than he can handle right now. One of the waitresses is leaving this weekend because she and her husband are moving to London and this morning, the head chef handed his notice in and to top it all, he had no gas in the kitchen."

"Oh, I know there was a gas leak in the village this morning. Everyone was talking about it; in fact, I saw a couple of British Gas vans when I went to the post office before going on to Mahjong and I could see Glebe Lane was cordoned off entirely. There were a couple of men digging up the road and two or three standing around, so I guess they were trying to locate and fix the problem."

"It did come back on before I left the restaurant, so that was no longer a problem for David, and I did manage to reassure him by letting him know that there's a possibility of redeploying staff from the York restaurant and telling him, failing that, he can get temporary staff until he finds suitable replacements."

"Surely, he didn't need you to tell him those things; after all, don't you pay him to manage the restaurant?"

"I do, but you know me, I like to keep my finger on the pulse when it comes to staffing issues, so they all know they must contact me when there are problems."

By this time Sui Ling was putting the dishes on the table, which included a soup, the stir-fry and rice and the two of them sat down to eat together.

"Do you remember the girl that was found dead in Bentham Woods when we were in Scotland, YK?"

"Vaguely, why?"

"Well, for the last two weeks, we've been talking about the case at Mahjong. Do you know it was never solved?"
"No, I didn't."

"Well, we girls have decided that we're going to do a little probing ourselves."

"Why on earth would you want to do that?"

"You know me, I don't like to see anything left unfinished and it seems the case is all but shelved. The police probably won't get involved again unless some new evidence is found and who knows, maybe we can be the ones to shed a little light sufficient at least to get the case re-opened. Also, I think because we're all mothers, well except for Cathy, and we have time to do a little investigating, we like the idea of helping for her parents' sake. I can't imagine what it must be like to lose a child and not know what really happened."

"It sounds a bit of a long-shot to me. If the police couldn't solve it, what makes you think you ladies can?"

"I don't know if we'll be able to, but we're all very interested in the case, especially Penny, who is our driving force, so we've agreed to give it a go."

"Okay, I guess you know what you're doing; just be careful. Is there any of that soup left? I'm still hungry."

"Yes, I'll get it for you and then I'm going to call Michael and Xiu Ying, as Harry should be home from school now, and I want to have a little chat with him."

"Say hello from me when you do because I've got to go back up to the office and finish going over the proposal for the new restaurant. Tell Michael I'll give him a call myself at the weekend."

Things were very different in Hazelby Manor, for Stella didn't have the opportunity to discuss the group's plans with her husband, Peter. She was sitting alone drinking her third glass of red wine. The dinner she'd prepared and had been keeping warm for almost two hours was drying out in the oven and she could only wonder at what might be delaying Peter this time. He had said he would be coming home to collect some papers this evening, so she had enthusiastically prepared a candlelit dinner for two, but it was turning out to be yet another futile attempt to put some spark back into their marriage. Her thoughts as to how they'd got to this stage were interrupted when her mobile phone started to ring.

"Sorry Stella, I got waylaid, so I'm not coming home tonight after all. I'm going to send a clerk over to pick up the papers I need tomorrow morning. Will you be home?"

"Yes," she said brusquely, but Peter didn't notice, or if he did, he chose to ignore her tone.

"They're on my desk in a large brown envelope with the words 'Laker vs Brown' on the label. There are a few other envelopes with case names on the outside too, so be sure to give him the right packet. I'll see you at the weekend. Bye."

And without a single loving word, he ended the call and she resigned herself to the fact that if their marriage was going anywhere, it was going down the tubes! She poured herself another large glass of wine, switched off the oven, filled her plate with food that didn't look in the least bit appetising anymore and flicked on the television.

In Little Hazelby, a different scene was playing out.

Gregory McKenzie was being his taciturn self as Penny informed him of her intentions to become a self-appointed private detective. She told him verbatim all about the case and what the Mahjong ladies had decided to do.

He broke his silence with the words, "It seems like a foolhardy plan to me Penny. I think you could find better ways to occupy your time. For a start, you could get a job. The school fees for the boys are a huge drain now that they're in senior school and some extra income would certainly help our financial situation."

Despite Gregory's NHS salary being topped up with income from his private practice, the mortgage on their five-bedroom home and the school fees for their twin boys took its toll on their finances. Their financial situation gave Gregory cause for concern because their savings had been pretty much depleted when Penny had suffered a mental breakdown after giving birth to the boys. Besides having to pay huge fees when she'd been admitted into a private hospital for almost six weeks, he'd also had to pay for psychiatric counselling for the whole of the following year and their savings had never recovered.

"I'm not going to go out to work. The boys are only eleven years old and when they're on holiday, I need to be here for them and not stuck in some dreary office, so you can forget that. Besides, I actually think what we're planning to do is a good thing or it will be if we solve the mystery."

"Oh, do what you want; you will anyway," sighed

Gregory.

The rest of their evening passed in silence as Gregory got stuck into doing the Times crossword and Penny put her nose in a book. Still, Gregory seemed uncharacteristically restless.

Chapter 4

The Sleuths Convene

On the day of their next game, Penny had already showered and had her first cup of coffee by seven-thirty in the morning. She'd set up the table, put out the tiles and was now making soup for lunch. Without a doubt, she was looking forward not only to their game but to discussing the murder case too.

No sooner had she finished cooking, than she heard Christmas chimes ring out and she headed to the door humming Good King Wenceslas. Her usual 'ding-dong' chimes had been replaced for the Christmas season with a doorbell that played carols.

As she opened the door, both Bailey and Toby raced past her and the two golden retrievers were out and rolling in the light covering of snow before she could even welcome her first arrival of the day.

"Come in, Sui Ling. Oh, my goodness, I can't believe it's starting to snow already. I love it, but I hope it doesn't settle just yet. It would be lovely to see on Christmas Day, but we could well do without it during the run up to the holiday with so many festivities coming up."

"Yes, the ground is already a little treacherous. I almost slipped over walking up your drive," replied Sui Ling.

Just as Penny was about to close the door, she saw Ruth's car pulling onto the drive with Cathy as a passenger, so she held it open a little longer and they both hurried in out of the cold.

"Bailey, Toby, come on!"

Both dogs bounded back into the house and Penny was quick to close the lounge door and shunt them both towards their beds at the back of the house to dry off. Penny then joined everyone in the lounge and offered them drinks.

"Girls, I have coffee ready and the kettle is boiling for tea. What would you all prefer?"

Everyone put in their orders and Cathy followed with appreciation for Penny's efforts at decorating for Christmas.

"I love your tree," she said. "It looks so real and you don't have all the pine needles that I have to contend with every year. Dan insists on buying a real tree because he says it reminds him of Christmas spent in his grandparents' cottage in the country. The whole family would spend every Christmas with the old folks, long gone now, of course, but he has very fond memories of them."

Penny responded wistfully, "I really miss coming downstairs every morning to the wonderful aroma of pine from a fresh tree too, as that always reminds me of my childhood. I'd love a real tree, but the pine needles would be a problem for Bailey and Toby, not to mention the cats."

"Where are the gorgeous Suky and Jenny today, Penny?" asked Ruth.

"Up on our bed as usual," Penny laughed. "They can't wait for us to get up in the morning so they can jump into our warm spots."

Sui Ling took their conversation back to the Christmas tree by saying, "I can't stand the mess of pine needles so I prefer an artificial tree, but I do like the smell of pine, which is why I buy those little pine sticks from the garden centre. I can get you some if you want, Penny, as I'm going there this week to pick up the poinsettias I've ordered."

"Oh, I'd love some. I meant to get some last year but never got around to it. Do you find them as good as the real thing?"

"If I'm honest, no, but they do give a whiff of pine if you get up close," said Sui Ling.

"Is Stella joining us today?" asked Ruth.

"I think so. I haven't heard otherwise," said Penny.

Right on cue the sound of 'O Little Town of Bethlehem' started to ring out and, once again, Penny headed to the door humming along.

"So sorry I'm late, Penny," said Stella as she brushed the light covering of snow from her jacket. "I had to stop off at the bank before heading here, but I come with a tasty treat because I stopped at Rosie's Bakery and picked up a half dozen mince pies for us."

"Oh, that is good news. Everyone loves a mince pie; in fact, I'd intended to bake some this week, but have been so busy with one thing and another, that I never got around to it. It's a wonder I found time to prepare lunch," she said, laughing.

"Let me get you a drink and then we can get down to business."

Before long, they were all seated in the lounge with hot drinks, and Penny opened the topic that had been on all of their minds since their last game.

"Well, I've spent hours at the library this week and have read all of the newspaper reports of the murder from the archives. So, I can tell you that the girl's name was Gemma Davies and she'd just turned twenty-two when she was found dead in the woods, apparently within hours of being murdered. Well, actually the report said she'd been dead for less than twenty-four hours. She was bludgeoned to death and, guess what, she was four weeks pregnant."

"Oh, no!" said Cathy. "That's awful."

"Well, there's a possible motive for her murder if ever there was one; a lover who didn't want a baby." said Sui Ling.

"George told me about the pregnancy too," said Ruth, "and he did say that there was no evidence of sexual assault, so that could possibly have been the motive."

"Oh, does that mean he's agreed to help us, Ruth?" Penny asked enthusiastically.

"Well, in a way. After a little pushing, he did say that he'd help by letting us know what amounts to public knowledge, but of course, we can get that information as Penny did from the archives. I really don't expect him to be able to tell us much; it would be more than his job's worth to give out confidential information, but I do believe he'll help us to fill in gaps here and there when he feels able."

"I really didn't get round to finding anything out, Penny," said Stella. "I'm still not totally sold on the idea, but I'll see how things go."

"Me too," agreed Cathy, "although I do feel so sorry for her knowing that she was pregnant. In fact, doesn't that make it a double murder?"

Ruth responded, "I don't think so, Cathy, because sadly, a foetus is not considered a person at such an early stage."

"Well, I think it should be," Cathy quickly responded. "When I get pregnant, I'll consider mine a baby from day one! So, what else do we know about her?"

Sui Ling took up Cathy's question. "I did my research on the Internet and found that she was from Armley in Leeds. Actually, she grew up quite close to the prison there. I also discovered that she was a beautician in a spa and that she was a popular, fun loving girl. She was an only child who seems to have come from a decent family."

Ruth added to the information to say that when Gemma was murdered, she was living away from home with a friend in an apartment near the city centre.

"So where do we go from here?" asked Cathy.

"Well, I think we need to continue to collect information so that we know exactly where to start," said Penny. "In fact, I also did a little digging in the village when I went to the hairdresser's; you know how Pamela, the hairdresser, loves to gossip. I did a little subtle probing and discovered that they didn't only question those with Range Rovers, they actually questioned a few men in the village. Two of them became serious suspects and were taken in for questioning more than once, but neither were charged."

"Oh, who were they?" asked Cathy.

"Well one was Charlie Statham who was in his late twenties at the time," Penny replied. "He was a bit of a loner and something of an oddball at the best of times. The other was an older man called Arthur Fisher, who lives alone on the outskirts of the woods where the girl was found by a young couple out walking their dog. Apparently, Arthur fitted the description of the man they said they'd spotted in the woods shortly before their dog found her body."

Ruth added to Penny's information, "Yes, Charlie was a suspect, primarily because he was known to the police for a few rather strange offences. Basically, he'd been found stealing women's underwear from washing lines on more than one occasion."

"Wow, he sounds like a real pervert!" said Cathy.

"He does," responded Sui Ling, "but there was obviously nothing to tie him to the case so they let him go. So, what happened with Arthur Fisher?"

"Well, they let him go too," said, Penny, "but both were considered suspects for a long time; in fact, there's talk in the village that either one of them could still have been guilty and just got away with murder."

Sui Ling added more information from her Internet search. "They also had suspects in the Leeds area. Her boyfriend was one, but she seems to have had many male friends because not only was she very pretty, but she was reported as being a very 'sociable girl' mixing in all kinds of circles, including some that were less than desirable. Although she worked in an up-market spa, the flat she shared with her girlfriend in town was not exactly in the most desirable area."

Stella, eager to start playing and still not quite on board with the plan for them to become amateur sleuths chimed in, "Are we going to play today or what?"

"Yes," said Penny, "of course. I've set up the table in the dining room already. Let's go and get started."

"How about we play the Western game today?" said Ruth.

"Oh, what a good idea," added Stella. "We haven't played the Western version for weeks; in fact, we'll all be forgetting the wonderful hands that are possible if we don't play again soon."

Cathy was quick to ask, "What do you mean by wonderful hands?"

"Oh, there are so many more hands in the Western game and their names are just delightful," replied Stella. "For example, there's 'Wriggly Snake', 'Three Philosophers' and how about this one, 'Moon at the Bottom of the Well.'"

"Oh, they are super names, but I remember playing before and it's definitely harder than the Chinese game. I don't think I can remember the simple hands let alone the wonderful ones!"

"I'll partner you to begin with, Cathy, until you get the hang of it," said Ruth.

"Oh, thank you; I need all the help I can get."

The next two hours passed in a flash as they all became engrossed in playing until they took a break to enjoy a bowl each of Penny's fresh vegetable soup with crusty bread followed by a mince pie and a glass of sherry.

Of course, during the break, their conversation returned to the topic of the murder and, more specifically, to what they might actually do to help solve the case. Penny was the first to raise the topic, as usual, and suggested a plan of action.

"Now that we know the major players, we need to dig into the detail and not just accept what we read. I think we ought to see if we can interview everyone involved because there are obviously still things to be discovered; otherwise, this case would have been solved already."

"Oh, Penny, don't you think that's a bit risky, especially as we might end up coming face-to-face with the murderer?" asked Stella.

"That's a good point, Stella," agreed Ruth, "I suggest we don't interview anyone alone, but instead always go together in twos. George would second that I'm sure, as he's concerned for our safety."

"Yes, that makes sense," said Sui Ling. "Would that put your mind at rest, Stella?"

"I guess so."

Cathy added, "It would certainly go some way to putting Dan's mind at rest as he's very against me getting involved because he thinks it's too risky, but it's something I really want to do, especially now that I know she was pregnant."

"To be honest, it's going to be very difficult for any of us to get moving on this given that Christmas is looming, not to mention all of the festivities that are coming up," said Ruth.

"Yes," agreed Sui Ling, "but it shouldn't stop us continuing to read everything that was printed at that time and keep our eyes and ears open for any tit bits we can gather from casual conversation in the community. That way, we'll be as ready as we can be to start interviewing those who were central to the initial investigation."

As soon as they were all happy with the plan, they headed back to the table and the only words that were then heard were the names of tiles being dropped one after another interspersed with, 'Pung', 'Chow', Kong', 'I'm fishing' and 'Mahjong'.

When the clock chimed three, their usual time to say farewell, Penny made a tempting offer for them to stay a little longer.

"Okay girls, this is the last game of the year for us, so I think we should have a Christmas drink together before we leave today. I've got a bottle of white open in the fridge and I'll get a nice bottle of red from Gregory's collection in the cellar, and we can all drink a toast in anticipation of a successful venture together before life gets super busy."

Everyone accepted her invitation and went to make themselves comfortable in the lounge.

Ruth was the first to speak about the upcoming festivities, by asking if any of them would be attending the village school's Nativity on Friday evening as she had been helping them to prepare for the event. Her role as Chair of the school governors gave her little choice, but she loved to be involved anyway.

"I'm sorry Ruth, but I won't be able to attend," said Penny. "Gregory and I have to drive up to the twins' boarding school on Thursday. They have their carol service just before the close of school and from there the four of us will be going on to spend the rest of the weekend with Gregory's family."

"Sorry, we won't be there either," said Sui Ling, "as YK and I already have a commitment that night, but I do hope it all goes well."

"No worries," said Ruth. "I understand how busy everyone is and how impossible it is to attend everything. I'm sure I'll see you both at the Golf Club Christmas Ball and maybe at the Carols by Candlelight service at the Church. Oh, and there's the pantomime, 'Jack and the Beanstalk', that the local amateur dramatic society are putting on twice next week too. Maybe I'll see some of you there."

"You can count on me being at the school on Friday, Ruth," said Stella, "but I wouldn't count on Peter joining me as he's more than likely to make work an excuse. If not we'll both be there, and of course we'll be at the Ball given Peter's role as the Golf Club President."

Cathy responded too, "Oh, I'd love to come, Ruth, and I'm sure Dan will come along as he's a big softie when it comes to all things Christmas. Do we need to buy tickets?"

"No, just come along at around five thirty, Cathy, and you'll be sure to find seats as it starts at six. We're going to be selling mulled wine and mince pies to the adults after the concert and we'll have hot chocolate and cookies available for the children too. This will all help with fundraising."

Sui Ling, responding to Ruth said, "YK and I will definitely be at the Ball, of course, and plan on coming to the church service too."

"Yes, we'll be at the Ball too, Ruth," said Penny, "and we also have tickets for 'Jack and the Beanstalk' on the first night. I'm sure the boys will love it. At eleven they're not too old to enjoy a good pantomime."

"Lovely," said Ruth. "I'm sure the twins will enjoy it. George and I are going on the first night too. It will be lovely to see the boys again and ask them about their first term as boarders."

"All of our paths will cross for sure, even though we won't be playing Mahjong again until January," said Sui Ling. "In fact, we should start playing again the week after your wedding anniversary, Ruth. Actually, that means we'll be playing on the 11th which is Penny's birthday. I think it will be my turn to host, so I can prepare a little birthday celebration."

"Oh, that's my birthday too," shared Cathy.

"Wonderful!" added Penny. "We can have a joint celebration."

Sui Ling agreed. "Yes, I'll prepare for a double celebration. In the meantime, girls, let's not forget our mission."

Chapter 5

The Festivities Begin

By four-thirty on Friday afternoon, the little village school was abuzz with children, teachers and parents preparing for the Nativity about to be performed. Ruth and a few of the volunteers were busy in the kitchen arranging the mince pies and that many parents had donated, while George was keeping himself busy making a huge pan of mulled wine.

All was going to plan until a loud crash rang through the school hall followed by the sound of loud gasps and crying. Everyone rushed out of the kitchen to find the stage Christmas tree lying on its side and little Freddie Harris standing beside it crying. He'd been tempted by the chocolate reindeers hanging on the tree and had tried to help himself to one that was just a little too far out of his reach.

A teacher was trying to console Freddie when George walked over, ruffled his hair and said, "That'll teach you not to help yourself to things that don't belong to you, young man."

George and Larry, the school caretaker, righted the tree and one of the parents got to work on sweeping up pieces of broken baubles that were scattered all around. Very soon the mess disappeared, everyone was seated and the stage curtains began to open revealing Miss Morris, the music teacher, seated at the piano with a group of children standing in the centre of the stage. Everyone applauded and, as soon as the curtains were fully open, Miss Morris began to play, 'Little Donkey' and the children sang the lyrics enthusiastically, albeit not always in tune. This heralded the start of the performance which included the audience being invited to sing along to the carols which were interspersed throughout the Nativity play.

Afterwards, while Ruth and Cathy were waiting for George and Dan to return with mulled wine and mince pies, Ruth spotted old Mr. and Mrs. Statham and gestured to Cathy to follow her as she made her way over to speak to them.

"How nice to see you both again; it's been a long time," said Ruth. "Cathy, let me introduce you. This is Mr. and Mrs. Statham."

They greeted each other and it didn't miss Cathy's attention that this was the same surname as the oddball they'd been talking about the other day. She immediately wondered if they were related, but the answer was soon provided by Ruth.

"How are you both and how is Charlie?"

Mr. Statham responded, "We're quite well Mrs. Cromwell, thank you."

Mrs. Statham was not quite so polite, for she chipped in quite quickly by saying, "We are, but the same can't be said for poor Charlie. I'll never forgive the gossipers for driving him away from his little flat here after the Bentham Wood murder, even though there was no evidence at all to say he was involved. I know my boy and he would never do such a thing."

Ruth knew that she'd opened up a wound that was obviously not healed in any way and she apologised.

"I'm so sorry for causing you distress. I didn't realise that it was still so painful for you."

"Do you mean to tell me that you wouldn't still be hurting if it had been one of your boys who'd been accused of murder and even when not charged had to suffer abuse and mockery from just about everyone around? Yes, we know Charlie had his problems, but today, people would be more understanding and he would receive help instead of hounding. In fact, everyone is encouraged to be who they want to be these days and, if a young man wants to dress in women's clothes today, I'm sure he wouldn't suffer as Charlie was made to do so twenty years ago.

"Yes, I'm still angry and I'll go to my grave being angry for he's become a recluse and so hard to reach not only because he now lives miles away in an isolated caravan, but also because he was never able to find a job after that. His life was ruined. In fact, I've no time for anyone here except the little innocents we've just watched performing. They remind me of how Charlie was once upon a time."

"As a mother, I really do understand how you must feel and again, I'm so sorry for bringing the pain to mind tonight. I do wish you both a merry Christmas and will pray for better times to come for you both and for Charlie."

Ruth and Cathy took their leave and joined George and Dan chatting with Stella, all with mulled wine and mince pies in hand.

"Wow, that was heavy, Ruth," said Cathy, "but although I feel sorry for her, I can't help but think she's so intense she could be just as passionate about covering for him too. Some parents would cover for their children no matter what they've done, even murder!"

Ruth and Cathy filled the others in on the interchange they'd just had with Mr. and Mrs. Statham. Dan was quick to agree with Cathy and shared that he found the whole underwear issue distasteful and could quite believe it possible that someone so strange might be capable of greater offences. He said that he and Cathy had watched many a crime programme which revealed how the activities of sick individuals can escalate and referred to the case of Ted Bundy in the US as an example.

George was quick to give an alternative view. "I understand what you're saying Dan, but to be honest, most petty criminals out there don't go on to commit murder."

Stella, despite having had only one mulled wine, was starting to slur her words a little. Ruth guessed she'd probably started drinking earlier in the day after Peter had told her he couldn't get home yet again, so Ruth decided to offer her a ride home. They all decided it was time to leave, so said their farewells until tomorrow when they would see each other at the Christmas Ball.

The following day, the hair and beauty salons all around

were fully booked and there was an air of excitement among all who were going to the Golf Club Ball that evening. By five o'clock, however, the shops had closed and there was little activity in the village, save for the snowflakes that had started to fall. The village seemed to sparkle as the snowflakes reflected light from the streetlamps and from the coloured bulbs on the village Christmas tree. Together, the snow and the lights with the pretty village backdrop created a scene worthy of a painting by Thomas Kinkade.

That evening when Cathy entered the Golf Club, she almost gasped aloud as she had never seen anything quite like it. The decorations were dazzling and with all of the men dressed in black tie and all of the ladies in evening gowns, it was a sight to behold. When she and Dan stepped onto the dais in the entrance to have their photographs taken by the side of the huge Christmas tree with a beautiful snow scene backdrop, she felt she'd been transported into some kind of magical wonderland.

"Oh, Dan, this is wonderful! Just look at those decorations," she said, pointing to hundreds of silver baubles hanging at various lengths from the ceiling and all linked with sparkling silver tinsel.

The walls of the room were covered in silver foil and the lights and candles on every table bounced reflections in all directions.

"Not quite like Christmas at my grandmother's cottage, but I'm not complaining," said Dan in his usual dry tone.

Cathy laughed. "I think you're looking at the past through

rose-coloured spectacles. Your mum has told me many times how bitterly cold it used to be out there with only a wood fire to keep you all warm. She said how the pretty, white landscape would quickly disappear when the rain turned the snow to slush and the damp would penetrate even the thickest layers of clothing. Yes, rose-coloured spectacles I believe!"

Dan was not about to have his childhood memories tainted, even by truth, so he simply gave her a wry smile before leading her towards the main room.

Shortly after entering, he excused himself and left Cathy to say hello to one of his contractors. He was not going to put business on hold, even though this was the social event of the year, but Cathy was not at all put out, for she was mesmerised by all that she could see. Besides, she'd already spotted Ruth crossing the room and coming towards her.

"My oh my, you look absolutely gorgeous in that emerald green gown. It looks stunning with your auburn hair, Cathy, and Dan looks so handsome in his tux."

"Thank you, Ruth. I love your dress too; you always look so elegant. Where's George?"

"He's around somewhere. We arrived early and we've been circulating ever since. Come, let me take you to our table."

Stella saw them both enter the main function room and straight away nudged Peter, who then excused himself from the young man he was talking to and the two of them headed over to greet Ruth and Cathy.

"Welcome ladies. What beauties my eyes behold!"

"Oh, Peter, ever the flatterer, but I'll take it tonight as I've made a bit of an effort," Ruth said laughingly.

Dan and George approached the little foursome at the same time and Peter warmly greeted the two of them with firm handshakes. "Good to see you both. Hope all is well with the boys in blue and down at the scrapyard."

He didn't give them time to answer before he called over a waiter and said, "Please help yourselves to champagne; there's no expense spared tonight as we're hoping you'll drink a lot and give a lot!"

Laughing at his own wisecrack, he made his excuses as he needed to circulate, but said that they'd talk later because he and Stella were seated at what he laughingly called 'The Big Mahjong table', given that all of the Mahjong ladies and their husbands were seated there together.

As he walked towards the door accompanied by Stella, Penny and Gregory were just coming into the function room and Peter greeted them both warmly.

Gregory responded in kind, but Penny simply said, "Peter," and then gave Stella a hug.

YK and Sui Ling were right behind them and, once again, Peter was the first to greet them.

Leaving Peter welcoming yet more guests, Stella ushered

both couples to the table where more greetings took place along with a generous dose of compliments being exchanged, particularly to Sui Ling who certainly stood out as the only lady in the room wearing a beautiful long cheongsam.

As soon as everyone had arrived and apéritifs had been served, Peter took to the stage and invited all guests to be seated. He then began his welcome address.

"On behalf of the Golf Club Committee, I want to say a warm welcome to each and every one of you for joining us this evening. I know you've already dug deep into your pockets to buy tickets for the evening in order to support our charitable endeavours, which, for the benefit of husbands whose wives have just dragged them here tonight, I'm talking about our plans to give to a variety of organisations who work to help those suffering from cancer. We'll be giving to research bodies as well as those who give practical help on a day-to-day basis. So, please dig even deeper tonight, buy lots of raffle tickets and put as many notes as you can into our big red postbox here on the stage because we're hoping to fill it to the brim. Now without further ado, I want to introduce our very own prize winning Hazelby String Quartet and to thank them for not only playing as we dine this evening, but also for giving freely of their time and talents to support our fundraising efforts."

On that note, the quartet began to play Vivaldi's Four Seasons Concerto No. 1 which provided a bright and cheerful welcome to the food. The first note was also taken as a signal to the bevy of waiters who then paraded out with trays held high in each hand before expertly placing one on each table from which the guests were then served their first course, a trio of dainty champagne and lemon prawn vol-au-vents.

The drinks flowed and the dinner was every bit as delicious as Stella had said it would be and, as dining gave way to dancing, the quartet was replaced by a local DJ who knew how to get everyone up on the floor. Some danced almost non-stop, but the Mahjong ladies also took time to listen and learn after subtly raising the topic of Gemma Davies from time to time.

It was old news as far as the community was concerned and some were puzzled as to why the topic was being raised again, but one man in particular had much to say when Penny and Sui Ling were chatting with him. This was Frank Cousins, the landlord of The White Hart. He knew a great deal about the case, maybe because tongues loosen when people have a few drinks inside them, especially those who sit at the bar chatting to the landlord and staff.

"I don't know why they couldn't find the guy who did it; there were enough clues," he said. "I think they closed the case too soon."

"What do you mean by 'clues'?" asked Sui Ling, "and how do you know that it was a guy?"

"Well, I can't be sure that it was a guy, of course, but there are more murders of women committed by men than by women. As for clues, there were the tyre tracks for a start, which they said were probably from a Range Rover, yet they didn't really follow up on that."

"They did, Frank," said Penny. "Stella told us that Peter had been questioned along with every other owner of a Range Rover for miles around."

"Oh, come on now, what good is questioning alone? Seriously, the murderer is hardly likely to say, 'Fair cop, it was me who did it', now is he? I think they spent far too much time chasing that young Charlie boy who never had two ha'pennies to his name, much less own a Range Rover. I know many around here thought he did it because, let's face it, he was a bit of a strange one, but I never did. To my mind, he never fitted the profile of a murderer.

"Then there was Arthur Fisher, who lives not far from the woods where she was found. He was a suspect for quite a while and many people thought it would turn out to be him, but the police were never able to pin anything on him either. I don't think he did it anyway. I think he was suspected just because he was a fifty odd year-old guy living alone near the scene of the crime, but that doesn't make anyone a murderer. After dismissing those two, the case focused more on the people she knew in Leeds and before long the whole thing just seemed to fizzle out and we never heard much after that."

"So, what's your view then, Frank? Do you have your own theory?" asked Penny.

"I do, lass; my guess is that it was some posh bloke with a Range Rover. Just because they didn't find him doesn't mean we don't have him living right here on our doorstep. Let's face it, this is one of the wealthiest villages around and it's well known that rich guys know how to cover their tracks or pay people to do so. Yes, my bet is that one day, we'll find out who did it and everyone around will be shocked, but not me; my money is on it being her sugar daddy living up here somewhere."

"Food for thought," said Sui Ling to Penny once they were able to speak alone again.

Penny replied by saying, "I think Frank's had a bit too much to drink, but he seemed coherent enough and we shouldn't dismiss what he said."

"I agree. We'll definitely share his thinking when we get together to decide on our next step after Christmas. Come on, let's get back to the others. I think I saw them heading outside, probably for a breath of fresh air, and I could do with some too because it's so warm in here now."

As the evening was drawing to a close, the big Mahjong table was full once again with the ladies and their husbands all enjoying a nightcap.

Peter was visibly happy as he spoke of the event. "Well, we really couldn't have wished for a more successful evening. I've received nothing but praise and thanks and have not received a single complaint! On top of that, we've raised a small fortune through the raffle and the post box is full of notes too! Harry and Gordon are in the office right now putting the proceeds in the safe and tomorrow we'll all count it, so it won't be long before we can announce how much has been raised."

Within half an hour, they were all bidding each other

farewell. Stella and Peter wished everyone in their little group a Merry Christmas and a Happy New Year as they knew they wouldn't see anyone again before leaving to spend Christmas in Paris with their son, Marcus. Dan and Cathy did the same as they had plans to travel to Sheffield to stay with Cathy's parents for the holidays in a couple of days so knew they wouldn't see their friends again this year either.

Christmas week in Hazelby began with the pantomime, Jack and the Beanstalk, being performed in the village hall. The school had already closed for the holidays and the annual pantomime was definitely one of the favourite events of the Christmas season for children and adults alike.

"Look behind you!" shouted the children as the giant appeared behind Jack, star of the pantomime. Jack responded to the children's call in super quick time and scooted down the beanstalk, which actually meant he disappeared down a trapdoor on the stage floor out of which a plastic beanstalk could be seen poking its head. It was a fun evening for the children and adults alike for they too joined in with the traditional pantomime shouts of, 'Oh, no, it isn't' and 'Oh, yes, it is' amid lots of laughter and, of course, they all enjoyed singing songs with the cast in the grand finale.

Once in the foyer, Ruth and George bumped into Penny and Gregory and their two boys, Felix and Jonathan.

Ruth was the first to speak. "Hello boys, how lovely to see you again. Did you enjoy the pantomime?"

The twins replied in unison, "Yes, thank you, Mrs. Cromwell."

"We enjoyed it too, didn't we George, and our boys used to love pantos when they were your age," said Ruth.

The men were exchanging a few words at the time so George didn't reply, but this didn't worry Ruth because she was already moving into conversation with twins first and then Penny.

"Will you all be at the Carols by Candlelight service on Christmas Eve, Penny?"

"No, we're hosting a Christmas Eve dinner for friends, so we won't see you again before Christmas. I'm really eager for our next Mahjong game though, because Sui Ling and I had a very interesting conversation with Frank Cousins at the Ball. We'll tell you all about it then because we need to hurry home now; we promised the boys pizza and I'm sure the delivery boy will be on his way already."

They all exchanged good wishes and Penny and Ruth gave each other a big hug before going their separate ways.

The church lights shone brightly in the darkness of night and acted like beacons to all heading to the Carols by Candlelight service on Christmas Eve. Ruth and George were at the door greeting everyone and handing out candles and wondering if they would have enough, for it seemed that not only Hazelby and Little Hazelby residents were attending, but people from surrounding villages too. There were certainly people there that they'd never met before, but they were not complaining; in fact, they both thought how wonderful it was to see the old church filling up once again.

Sui Ling and YK arrived and, like everyone else, received a warm welcome from Ruth and George. George told Ruth that he could deal with any latecomers and suggested she escort them to the seats he'd reserved so they could all sit together. No sooner had they reached their seats, however, than YK excused himself to go to the bathroom. Ruth, who had been burning to talk to Sui Ling ever since her conversation with Penny, took the opportunity to do so.

In a hushed voice, Ruth said, "I've been so intrigued by a conversation I had with Penny the other day because she told me you'd both had a very interesting chat with Frank Cousins, but she had to rush and couldn't say anything more at the time. What did you discover?"

Replying in an equally soft voice, Sui Ling briefly shared Frank's view and both agreed that his theory was sufficiently interesting to give them a starting point for their investigation. YK returned just as the organ burst into life and together the three of them stood lifting their voices to the music of 'Hark the Herald Angels Sing', along with the rest of the congregation.

Chapter 6

The Christmas Day Celebrations

On Christmas morning, Cathy and Dan woke with a start to the shouts of, "He's been, he's been, Father Christmas has been!" Dan looked at the clock and groaned as it was only five thirty in the morning. He wanted to roll over and go back to sleep, but Cathy seemed as excited as her seven-year-old niece, Rosie, and five-year-old nephew, Billy. Pulling on her dressing gown she encouraged Dan to get up too, "Come on Dan we don't want to miss the little ones opening their Christmas presents."

The household, in Sheffield, quickly burst into life as the children's shouts of glee had also woken Cathy's parents, Doreen and Barry, as well as the parents of the energetic twosome, Cathy's sister, Jackie, and her brother-in-law, Stephen.

In Little Hazelby, however, Penny and Gregory's morning had got underway when their eleven-year-old twins, Felix and Jonathan, woke them at the more reasonable time of seven a.m. It didn't take them long to open their presents though because Penny and Gregory were not ones to spoil their children with too many gifts. In fact, this year, the boys had both received mountain bikes which they'd assembled in super quick time with their dad.

Penny called to them from the kitchen, "Come on, you guys. It's time for breakfast. If you're going out for a good ride this morning, you'll need some hot food inside of you; it's bitterly cold."

In no time at all, they'd wolfed down their cooked breakfast and were heading out of the door to test ride their new bikes.

"Don't be late back; remember we're eating at one o'clock."

Meanwhile, in Newcastle, at Edwin and Margie's home, where Sui Ling and YK were spending the Christmas weekend, a late breakfast was being enjoyed. Their daughter, Candy, however, was missing from the table as she had arrived quite late from her home in the staff quarters of Caledonia University the previous evening and was still in bed.

"If she's not up in the next hour, I'm going to wake her Margie," said Sui Ling, "as we promised Michael, we'd call them before they go out for dinner at six, and it's already three o'clock in Shenzhen."

"Good idea! Meanwhile, let's get started on preparing the veggies for tonight."

The two of them cleared the breakfast dishes away as YK and Edwin, already talking business, took their leave.

Back in the village of Hazelby, in Ruth and George's thatched cottage, a double celebration was underway because it was not only Christmas Day but Ruth's birthday too. Ruth and her sister-in-law, Judy, had been in the kitchen, almost from waking, preparing the turkey, vegetables and all of the other traditional goodies that would grace the table later in the day. Ruth and George had invited Ruth's mum, Audrey, and Ruth's brother, Matthew, and his wife, Judy, brought her with them having arrived just as the Carol concert was finishing the previous evening. John, Ruth and George's eldest son and his wife, Becky would also be joining them for lunch.

At ten o'clock precisely, the recognisable sound of a Facetime call rang out and Ruth became very excited as she knew it would be Tom, their youngest son, who was a junior officer in the British Army.

"Hello Tom, how's it going out there?"

Ruth could hear George already talking to their son and she quickly dried her hands and hurried through to the lounge.

"Yes, she's here now," George said and he passed his phone over to her.

"Happy birthday, mum! I really wish I could be with you all today, but at least we've got good Internet over here, so I don't need to miss out on talking to you. I asked John and Becky to pick up a present I ordered for your birthday so they'll be bringing it with them later today. I couldn't send you a card from here either, so I'm afraid you'll have to be satisfied with an e-card this year. Check your email as soon as you can."

"Oh, Tom, it's so lovely to hear your voice. I miss you so much, but I'm so proud of you and what you are doing over there."

Tom was on the phone for the next hour, for not only did Ruth and George chat with him, but so did his Uncle Matthew and Aunt Judy and his Grandma Audrey.

In complete contrast to her four friends, Stella slept until almost noon in Paris. She'd had a restless night waking several times and had even found herself staring out of the window at three o'clock in the morning for almost an hour. Sadly, not even the perfect view of the Eiffel Tower that she and Peter had, gave her any joy, for despite being in the city of romance, she felt as neglected and alone as she did at home. In fact, at this very moment, she had no idea where Peter was. Still, she looked forward to their dinner with Marcus that evening and meeting the friend he'd said would be joining them for dinner.

Christmas Day passed very differently for each of the Mahjong ladies. By early afternoon, in Sheffield, the Cathy and Dan Skidmore's day was in full swing and as noisy as it had been when it had started. This was because Dan's children from his first marriage, teenagers Mark and Lucy, had been added into the mix and all four children were playing Twister and making enough noise for ten as they laughed and fell over each other.

In the kitchen, the adults chatted as dinner was being prepared, but Cathy was taken aback when Dan suddenly said, "Barry, what do you think of this madcap idea of your daughter's to become a crime fighter?"

"Thanks, Dan! It's a good job I've already talked to them about it. I'm not a child and don't need their permission or yours, so stop trying to get support for your objections."

Barry, in an attempt to head off what could turn into a Christmas spoiler, said, "Come on you two; let's not go down this path today. The only thing I would say, Cathy, is to watch your step. I do share Dan's concern for your safety, so don't take any unnecessary risks, okay?"

"Okay, okay, I'm not planning to, so let's drop this now," she replied.

Dan agreed and, in order to cool things down said, "Okay, guys, I think it's time for a movie. I've got everything set up for us to watch 'Polar Express' unless anybody fancies their chances against me at Monopoly!"

Peace was restored and there was no more tension for the rest of the day. Movies were watched, dinner was enjoyed, games were played and when the youngsters were in bed, the adults enjoyed a drink and played cards together to round off their evening.

Back in Little Hazelby, Penny had been keeping the Christmas lunch warm for the past hour because Gregory and the boys had still not returned. She could see that Gregory had left his mobile on the hall table, so she knew ringing him was not an option. However, just as she was beginning to wonder if she should be worried, she saw the three of them coming up the drive. Far from being relieved though, she felt angry when they walked in because Gregory didn't even think to apologise for being late.

"That was fantastic! It was bitterly cold up on the moors, but we all got a pace on and very soon, we didn't even feel it. Just look at the boys!"

Penny could see their cheeks were flushed and both were smiling from ear to ear, so for their sake, she held her tongue and just told them to get washed up because she was ready to serve. The boys devoured their dinner in short order, not just because they were starving after mountain biking for almost four hours, but because they wanted to get back to their computer games.

Gregory and Penny sat across from each other in an uncomfortable silence after the boys left; at least that's how Penny felt. Gregory, on the other hand, was typically oblivious to her mood. If he hadn't been, he might never have opened his mouth.

"Penny, I'm still not happy about you becoming involved in this amateur detective thing. Are you still planning to go ahead with it?"

"Of course, why would I have changed my mind?" Penny snapped. "Anyway, what's it to you? I'm not asking you to be involved."

Gregory in a somewhat uncharacteristic way, seemed to want to push his own agenda on the matter, which Penny noted, but couldn't understand.

"Well, besides putting yourself at risk, it seems to me to be just opening up old wounds which could cause a lot of people pain without any guarantee that you can do any good. I know, I know, I can't tell you what to do, so don't shout me down, but I've got a bad feeling about all this and I really wish you would find something else to occupy your time."

"That's so patronizing! This is not something we're doing just to pass our time. We're all quite driven and who knows, maybe we'll unearth some buried secrets that lead to the case being solved because somebody out there knows more than they're saying."

Almost inaudibly, Gregory muttered, "That's what I'm afraid of."

Penny rounded on him immediately, "What's there to be afraid of? You sound like you don't you want us to find out who did this."

"Of course, I want whoever is responsible to be brought to justice; I just don't want my family involved. Look, forget I said anything. Shall we get the boys off their computers and watch 'Elf' together; they love that movie."

Glad of an escape from her own tension as well as this conversation, she readily agreed. "All right, you go and find the DVD while I set the dishwasher going."

The movie did all that the two of them had hoped for, but for different reasons, and they then went on to enjoy the rest of the day, first by playing a very long game of 'Risk', which Gregory's parents had bought Felix for Christmas and then, a couple of games of 'Ticket to Ride', which they'd bought for Jonathan. After the boys had gone to bed, Gregory had more sense than to raise the subject of the murder again and he and Penny simply enjoyed a little supper together as they watched 'National Lampoon's Christmas Vacation', an all-time favourite of theirs.

In Newcastle, Sui Ling and her family were all seated with their eyes glued to the television.

"Hello, Michael, Merry Christmas!" Sui Ling and YK gave identical greetings almost simultaneously as Michael's face appeared on screen. Sui Ling quickly asked, "Where's Xiu Ying and Harry?"

"They're coming. Oh, here they are now!"

Suddenly the television screen, which had been connected to a computer for the Christmas Day family call, was filled with the faces of the whole family and, in China, the screen in Michael and Xiu Ying's home projected the faces of Sui Ling, YK, Edwin, Margie and Michael's sister, Candy.

They all shared their news and plans for the holiday and, of course, much attention was given to Harry who, at three, was feeling Christmas excitement for the very first time. As always, the time passed very quickly and before they knew it, Michael was starting to bid them farewell, but Candy interrupted.

"Don't go yet. Let me tell you my good news because it means you're going to be seeing me a lot sooner than you thought. I've had a paper accepted for presentation at a medical conference in Beijing in February and I'm going to travel via Shenzhen so that I can spend a few days with you guys too."

Everyone was thrilled and the call finished on a high note with a few plans already made for the visit.

The rest of their day passed just as pleasantly. Candy talked enthusiastically about her work as a medical researcher and they ate a sumptuous dinner together before eventually, and not surprisingly, YK and Edwin started talking shop again. The ladies were happy to leave them to it and took their tea into the sitting room where Sui Ling took the opportunity to share her Mahjong group's plan.

Just as she expected, both were supportive and Margie laughingly said, "Let me know if I can be of any help. I've always fancied myself as a bit of a detective."

Back in Hazelby with all the family gathered, Ruth also shared the ladies' plan. Her son, Matthew urged caution, but his wife, Becky, also on the force, took a more positive view because she knew from her own experience how valuable public involvement can be, especially when cases have gone cold. However, this news was soon to be overshadowed.

As they sat down to dinner, Becky handed round home-made Christmas crackers which everyone pulled immediately. George was the first to put his Christmas cracker hat on, but Ruth was the first to read the joke; only it wasn't a joke. Instead of the usual corny script, Ruth found herself reading, 'Congratulations, you are going to be a grandma!' She couldn't have been more excited if she'd tried. She whooped with joy and was up in a flash giving both Matthew and Becky big hugs. By this time everyone else had read their messages and congratulations were ringing in the air.

The rest of their day passed with lots of talk about the impending arrival in May and was rounded off with their traditional Christmas Day viewing of the movie, 'It's a Wonderful Life'.

The last of the ladies to get ready for Christmas dinner was Stella in Paris. She was showered and dressed by the time Peter walked in.

"Where have you been?" she fired at him.

"You were out like a light so I decided to go and have breakfast alone and then take a walk down by the Seine. What time is Marcus expecting us?"

"He said any time after five o'clock, so we've got plenty of time. I actually want to ring home and wish Brenda and Eric a Merry Christmas and check that all is well with the house before we go, so I'll do that now."

Peter poured himself a drink as Stella called her housekeeper. "Hello, who's that? Oh, Jack, hello, I didn't recognise your voice. Merry Christmas! Is your mother there? Okay, no worries; I'll call again in half an hour."

As she put down her phone, she knew Peter would not be too pleased that Jack was back on the scene.

"All right before you go into another rant about the 'layabout' as you call him, I'm sure he'll only be home for Christmas; besides, he is their son after all."

"Well as long as they keep the keys to our place away from the light-fingered layabout! I just hope it is only a short visit and that he isn't there when we get back."

"He probably won't be as he only ever visits them when he wants something and leaves as soon as he gets what he wants. Poor Brenda and Eric, as soon as he gets what he wants from them, he'll be off again."

By four forty-five, they were in a cab wending their way through the Paris streets to their son's home with their Christmas gift in hand: two tickets to an opera at The Palais Garnier was Stella's idea of a gift as she didn't know anything about her son's friend and it certainly wouldn't have been right to go there with only a gift for Marcus. Within twenty minutes, they were being warmly welcomed by their son and introduced to his friend, Sebastian.

As if there wasn't enough tension between Peter and Stella given their strained relationship, Stella knew tonight would heighten it because it was obvious to her that Sebastian was more than a just a friend. She eyed Peter cautiously wondering if he had caught onto that fact as well and from, his demeanour, she knew, without a doubt, he had, which she also knew would mean tonight would be difficult.

Gifts were exchanged and Stella tried to keep the conversation light and flowing. She could see that Peter was trying, but he really couldn't hide his distaste for the relationship that had caught him totally unawares. She had no problem with it herself; she just wanted her son to be happy, but she knew that Peter would struggle to deal with it; he'd probably have preferred Marcus to be a serial womaniser rather than what he'd been confronted with tonight.

To try and break the tension a little and keep the conversation flowing after dinner, she decided to tell everyone about what she and the Mahjong ladies were about to do, but, if she thought that would help, she couldn't have been more wrong.

"What! Are you mad?" boomed Peter. "Why on earth would put yourself at risk of harm from some lunatic out there and risk bringing our village back into the news? For goodness sake, it was bad enough when the case was active and all eyes were focused on us. The last thing we need is all this raked up again!"

His eyes bulged and his nostrils flared as he delivered his words so angrily and, Marcus, while sympathetic to his father's seeming care for his mother, had no warm feelings towards him tonight, for his attitude made it clear that he didn't like Sebastian.

Marcus quickly rose to her defence by saying, "I think it's a good thing to want to get to the bottom of something so horrendous as that girl's murder. I was only seven at the time, but I remember it happening. Surely, if the group is careful, no harm should come to them. As for the village being back in the news, I don't think that compares to the possibility of them actually uncovering something that leads to finding the girl's murderer."

Not for the first time, Marcus felt the wrath of his father's tongue.

"Keep your opinions to yourself. You don't have to live there and it's obvious that you and I have very different views on what is right and wrong!"

At that, Stella said, "I think it's time for us to leave. Thank you both for a lovely dinner. It was a pleasure to meet you Sebastian, and I'm sorry that I raised this issue which ended up spoiling the evening."

Sebastian responded in his heavy French accent, "It was a pleasure to meet you Madame, and I look forward to meeting you again one day. Au revoir!"

Peter had totally lost his usual impeccable manners and walked out without so much as a backward glance let alone any niceties. Stella hugged both young men and simply said she would be in touch and then quickly followed Peter out of the door.

In the cab on the way back to their hotel, not a word passed between them. It had not turned out to be anything like the day Stella had hoped for and imagined.

The days between Christmas and the New Year were filled with traditional activities for all but Stella and Peter. Ruth and George enjoyed good food and a few gentle walks with their family every time the winter sun made an appearance. Penny and Gregory took advantage of the brighter days to take their twins and dogs for a couple of vigorous hikes on the moors. Games and movie watching continued to be the order of the day for Cathy and Dan and their family in Sheffield while Sui Ling's family mixed work with pleasure because on Boxing Day the men headed back to their offices. On the less bright days, when the sun was more notable for its absence than its warmth, the outdoors became the place most avoided. Those who did venture out, such as Gregory and Penny to walk their dogs, found themselves having to endure the bitter North wind. It blew ice-cold rain and sleet in all directions stinging faces and somehow managing to penetrate even the warmest of outdoor wear.

Chapter 7

The New Year

Despite the near freezing temperatures across England, New Year's Eve dawned bright and sunny and this lifted everyone's spirits creating an air of optimism for the year ahead.

The New Year for Sui Ling, YK, Ruth and George got off to a fine start. Celebrating together at the Edinburgh Green Dragon, they were treated to a Scottish Hogmanay with a Chinese twist. Haggis served side-by-side with Peking duck and, of course, in good Scottish tradition, as the clock struck twelve, everyone stood and linked arms to sing Auld Lang Syne. The foursome then wished each other a Happy New Year amid much noise and celebration as friends and strangers moved around hugging each other and exchanging New Year greetings.

As the clock struck twelve in Little Hazelby, Penny, Gregory and the twins also stood to sing Auld Lang Syne. It was the first year that Felix and Jonathan had been allowed to stay up on New Year's Eve, but, after hugs and good wishes, Penny quickly shooed the boys off to bed. They'd been wilting since ten o'clock and she knew that if she didn't get them upstairs quickly, either Gregory would end up having to carry them to bed or they'd have to leave them sleeping on the sofas. Penny and Gregory followed the boys after enjoying a quiet nightcap together.

Cathy and Dan had arrived home in time for the New Year and they were also celebrating, but more than just the fact that this was a new year, for that morning Cathy had done a pregnancy test and it had confirmed what she'd been hoping for since Christmas Day. She was pregnant and from the minute she knew, she could talk of nothing else. Dan was equally happy because he'd suspected that the next step for them would be fertility treatment, something that he'd not relished. At two minutes to midnight Dan offered Cathy a glass of wine to toast the New Year, but Cathy was having none of it and she asked him to give her a glass of fresh orange juice instead. She'd waited long enough for this pregnancy and was not about to do anything that she considered harmful for the baby.

The only home in which New Year celebrations were not taking place was Stella's. In fact, she was alone because Peter had left for Leeds on the 28th and had not returned. He had not even told her when he would be back and, as the clock struck twelve, she just took another gulp of wine and, with tears filling her eyes, she could only wonder why everything was such a mess.

Upon their early return from Paris after a disastrous Christmas Day, things had just gone from bad to worse! As soon as they'd opened their own front door, they'd found themselves face-to-face with Jack.

"What are you doing here?" Peter had immediately snapped. "I've made it very clear you're not welcome here, so get out and don't come back!" he'd shouted.

Stella knew he had no time for Jack, but this outburst was

just so out of character because Peter was always at pains to present himself as in control and amiable. Normally, his reputation seemed more important to him than anything else, but not this time.

The commotion had obviously reached Brenda's ears because she was quick to appear on the first-floor landing and then come hurrying down the curved staircase. She was apologising profusely before she'd even reached the bottom step because she knew that Jack was not welcome in the house and she was the one who'd invited him in.

"I'm so sorry, I just asked Jack to help me carry some firewood indoors because Eric is not too well and I wanted to prepare for your return. I didn't expect you back today and he was just about to leave."

This did not satisfy Peter who was quick to respond, "When I said he's not to come into my house, I meant it and you have no right to invite him in behind my back. I don't trust him, and you know that!" he added.

"I know, Sir, but he's not a wild teenager anymore. He's settled down and is working in Leeds. He only stayed on with us after Christmas because of Eric being unwell," Brenda explained.

Stella was more than a little puzzled that Jack didn't seem at all perturbed by Peter's anger, but rather stood back with what could only be described as something of an impassive look on his face. As if that wasn't puzzling enough, she was taken aback when she heard him speak to Peter.

"Calm down, old man. I think you and I need to have a little talk. We've got some unfinished business to discuss. We can do it here or in private," she heard him say.

Peter had paled and, much to Stella's surprise, instead of ordering Jack out again, through gritted teeth, he'd said, "Okay, come into my office and let's get this over and done with. I haven't got time to waste on you."

Stella and Brenda had stood together in the empty hallway after Jack and Peter had disappeared into the office and the big oak door had been closed behind them. Neither of them understood what they had just witnessed and Brenda had quickly excused herself saying that she'd better check on Eric. Stella had then gone into the lounge and poured herself a drink before she headed upstairs with her travel bag to unpack.

Inside the office, Peter was the first to speak, "What are you doing back and what do you mean by saying we've got unfinished business and in front of my wife too? I've told you you're getting nothing else from me!"

"I know what you said, but I'm in trouble and need a helping hand. I need to find £5000 and quickly," Jack replied.

"What!" Peter exclaimed. "I've told you before, you're getting nothing more out of me."

"Look I'm in a fix and you're the only one who can bail me out. It's a matter of life and death and I'm not ready to die just yet."

"You've had more than enough from me, Jack. Besides, do you think I keep that kind of money around at home?"

"I know, but you can get it, right?" Jack responded. "I'll meet you wherever you want and I'll not bother you again," Jack replied, "and then, I'll head straight back to Leeds on the next train."

"So much for staying on here to help your parents," said Peter, "You've really got them fooled, haven't you? It's very clear that I, or rather my money, was the only reason you hung around this long."

Nevertheless, feeling backed into an old corner, Peter had reluctantly agreed.

"Okay, I'll meet you in the car park at the back of the White Hart at one o'clock tomorrow and, after I hand it over, I don't want to see you back here again. Do you understand?"

Jack nodded and left without another word.

Stella had no idea what had taken place. All she knew is that two days later, Peter had packed a bag and said he'd got to go to Leeds and would be in touch, but she'd not heard from him for three days.

During the first few days of the New Year, as common practice would have it, resolutions were being broken, but that seemed to be of little concern to anyone as the main topic of conversation among ladies in both villages was how to lose the weight they'd gained over Christmas. However, with Ruth and George's 30th wedding anniversary celebration on the horizon, diets were no more than a short-lived activity for those invited to the event.

On the 8th of January, the church bells rang out and onlookers that afternoon would never have guessed this was a renewal of vows service as it looked to all intents and purposes as if a full-blown wedding was taking place.

A vintage car pulled up outside the church and out stepped a 'bride' and 'groom' looking as happy as if it was their actual wedding day. Ruth looking stunning in her gown with George looking handsome and distinguished by her side. Family and friends added to the air of celebration as they'd been arriving from far and wide dressed in their finest.

The old Hazelby Methodist Church was packed and as the rich sound of the pipe organ, which had pride of place at the front of the church, burst into life with the hymn 'Praise My Soul the King of Heaven' even those outside on the village green could hear it. Inside, the sun shone through the stained-glass windows creating an appearance of droplets of colour everywhere.

As soon as the hymn came to an end, the organist began to play 'Jesu, Joy of Man's Desiring' and George was given the signal to enter the church. He did this with Ruth on his arm and, through the mists of time, both were instantly transported back to the day when they had walked down this very aisle separately and left together as man and wife.

The service was very special and moving for them both and, though Ruth's father was missing, her brother, Matthew, spoke of him and how proud he would have been of the two of them. He also spoke of the couple's love for each other and shared that their marriage had provided a model for many to follow, including his and Judy's.

The ceremony itself was led by their very old friend, Reverend Sean Trayford, who had been in Sunday school with Ruth when her father was the minister. Who would have imagined back then that one day he would be conducting a renewal of vows service for her, certainly neither of them!

The service closed with all voices raised to sing 'Amazing Grace' before everyone followed the bride and groom out of the church and onto the village green, which was bathed in perfect winter sunshine as if ordered especially for the day. Photographs were taken and shortly afterwards, those invited to the reception headed to the Golf Club.

Stella, Cathy, Sui Ling and Penny and their husbands enjoyed welcome drinks together and then found a table to share when John, Ruth and George's son, invited everyone to be seated. After a welcome speech by John who spoke with pride about his parents and life growing up with them, he asked everyone to raise their glasses in a toast to the happy couple. George responded by thanking everyone for coming and then invited them to enjoy themselves. The formalities over, it was announced that the buffet was now open.

Everyone enjoyed the delicious fare and, before long, the men, who were seated together at one side of the table, became engrossed in conversation. At the other side of the table, the ladies returned to the topic uppermost in their minds, well, except for Cathy's mind, but, as she and Dan had agreed, they must wait another month or so before telling anyone their good news. She knew she couldn't break it yet.

"I cannot wait until we meet on Tuesday morning," said Penny. "I've been doing bits of research in between all of the festivities and I discovered that there were a small number of people who actually admitted to killing the girl in the months following her murder. Investigations discovered none of them to be telling the truth."

"What!" asked Cathy. "Why on earth would anyone admit to a crime they'd had nothing to do with?"

Sui Ling joined the conversation, "It's not as unusual as you think, Cathy. It happens quite often, and studies show the reasons to be varied. One is a wish for notoriety at any cost, obviously."

Stella interjected, "What a waste of police time. I remember the case of 'Wearside Jack' who did the same thing. He claimed to be the Yorkshire Ripper by sending a number of letters and an audio recording to the police about murders of prostitutes in the 1970s. They eventually caught him, but it was years later."

"Yes, I remember that case," said Sui Ling, "It took almost thirty years for the police to track him down, which was long after the Yorkshire Ripper, who Wearside

Jack was pretending to be, was caught. Actually, the Ripper was arrested in your old hometown of Sheffield, Cathy. Thinking back on that case, which led to the biggest manhunt in UK history, we should all be encouraged in our desire to solve the Bentham Woods murder because, despite many experienced officers working on the Yorkshire Ripper case, one of the two officers who ended up arresting him was a rookie. It just goes to show that experience is not always necessary when it comes to solving crimes."

"Talking of Sheffield, when Dan and I headed there for Christmas, we had to drive past Bentham Woods and I saw the cottage where I think the old guy, Arthur Fisher, lives. There was smoke coming out of the chimney, so he was obviously at home, and I really wanted to stop and start asking him questions, but I knew for sure Dan wouldn't have entertained such an idea if I'd have raised it with him," she said laughingly. "Still, I'd love to be the one who gets to talk to the old man once we get going with this though. Of course, with someone else, as I know we've got to do everything in twos once we get started."

At that point, Ruth and George, who were doing the rounds, came to their table to thank them all for coming. This stopped all conversation and despite the ladies being eager to share with Ruth what they'd just been discussing, they all knew this wasn't the time or the place.

In fact, the conversation couldn't continue anyway, as the minute Ruth and George had said 'thank you', the 'Anniversary Waltz' began to play and the DJ called them both up for the first dance. As soon as that finished, despite the ladies having a strong desire to return to the topic which was preoccupying them, the DJ revved up the noise level which stopped all but one-to-one conversations. This was clearly the time for dancing and not talking, and Greg and Penny, who liked to strut their stuff on the dance floor, were the first to leave their seats. One by one, the remaining three couples rose to dance too, and the rest of the evening passed most pleasurably.

At ten p.m., Cathy, conscious of not wanting to overdo things, suggested to Dan that they should leave and the two of them bid everyone goodnight. By eleven, it was time for everyone else to say their goodnights and, as the ladies parted ways, Sui Ling reminded them that their first Mahjong game of the year would be held at her home on Tuesday morning.

Chapter 8

The Plan

Sui Ling had decorated her lounge with a banner and balloons, and the cake she'd ordered from the village bakery was already on the coffee table awaiting the arrival of the birthday girls, Cathy and Penny. No sooner had she stepped back to give the room one last check than the doorbell rang and she found Ruth and Stella on the doorstep. They'd agreed to come early to help with the preparations, but Sui Ling, in her usual organised way, had everything ready and waiting, so the three of them headed straight to the kitchen for a morning coffee.

"I'm so looking forward to getting down to business today and actually starting to take action. I think we've done more than enough research and talking," said Sui Ling.

"Oh, I think the birthday girls are here," Stella interrupted. "I've just heard a car door closing."

Within seconds, the ding-dong of Sui Ling's doorbell broke the silence as they listened and proved Stella to be right. All three hurried to the front door and as soon as Sui Ling opened it, they chimed in unison, "Happy birthday!"

Hugs quickly followed and once again the Mahjong ladies were united for a whole morning of uninterrupted games and, of course, the start of their murder investigation. With drinks in-hand they all sat down to enjoy watching

Penny and Cathy opening the gifts that Sui Ling had bought for them on behalf of the group. Everyone began to laugh when they both opened their boxes to find a magnifying glass, a notebook and pen and a flashlight: fun gifts in keeping with their soon-to-be detective roles.

Ruth had held her news to herself since first arriving, but she could no longer hold it and announced to one and all that she was an expectant grandmother. She filled them in on the impending arrival and congratulations, once again, resounded around the room.

At this point, Cathy struggled to keep her pregnancy a secret; she so wanted to tell them all, but she knew that if she shared it, she'd be breaking the agreement she had with Dan. They had both agreed to keep the news to themselves until she had passed the twelfth week. This alone, enabled her to resist the temptation to share.

After the congratulations and the baby talked ceased, the five of them were so eager to focus upon the case that they decided to talk about it before having their first game.

"So, let's take a few minutes to remind ourselves of what we know about the case so far," said Penny, taking the lead.

"Good idea," agreed Sui Ling. "I'll make notes on my laptop as we talk and then email them to each of you."

"Perhaps you could be our recorder of information throughout our investigation?" Ruth asked.

"I'll be more than happy to do that," Sui Ling replied and, with her laptop balanced neatly on her lap, she recorded the information as they shared.

Ruth was the first to contribute. "Well, we do know that the original search began in and around our area before it moved to Leeds."

"Yes," added Stella, "and I know from personal experience that all Range Rover owners around here were questioned at the time, but that the only suspects from hereabouts were Charlie Statham and Arthur Fisher. For some reason, neither of them was ever charged."

"Well, that could be because they were not guilty." Cathy was quick to offer.

"Yes, it may well be," Penny responded, "but I don't think we should accept anyone as being innocent. I think we should start from scratch without preconceived ideas and begin by questioning everyone who will talk to us, especially those most connected with the case."

"I agree," said Ruth. "I think we should draw up a list of those we want to talk to and then decide which of us will interview them."

"We should include people like the hairdresser, Pamela Shaw, and the landlord, Frank Cousins, because they could be holding some hidden gems given that they both talk to so many people and seem to know everyone's business," added Stella.

"I agree," said Penny. "Customers always talk to them and

both are always eager to talk to anyone who will listen so they may well have information worth hearing."

"We need to talk to people she knew in Leeds too," added Cathy. "There was her ex-boyfriend; we definitely need to speak to him and also to her flatmate at the time. Although I feel I should offer to do Leeds interviews because I used to live there, in all honestly, I'm not sure that would be an asset these days as I was only sixteen when I left. In the last few years, I've actually had difficulty finding my way around whenever I go to visit because things have changed so much."

"I can understand that!" agreed Ruth. "I have trouble finding my way around too, and I've been visiting for years. I don't think it matters who goes. Perhaps we should each just interview those we feel drawn to. I'd actually like to go there to speak to her parents, but I'll have to tread very carefully. I would hate to upset them, like I managed to do with Charlie's parents at Christmas."

"Yes, they'll be a good source of information about others in her past such as friends who may not have featured so publicly in the original investigation," added Sui Ling. "I think you have a point about not wanting to upset people though, but this links to another problem we might have because it's possible that not everyone will be willing to speak to us because there's no reason why they should."

"Absolutely, we'll need to exercise all of our social and interviewing skills to get people to open up to us," Ruth agreed.

"I think they'll be only too ready to speak to us when they know we only want to see justice being done," piped up Cathy.

"All except the murderer of course!" Stella laughingly replied.

"Well, if anyone refuses to cooperate, I think we should just put them on our suspect list straight away," Cathy said.

"Ah, if only it were that easy, Cathy," commented Stella. "There may be many reasons why people are reluctant to talk to us. Another thing that crosses my mind is that one of our biggest challenges might be locating people after so many years."

"That's true and that reminds me, we need to find the young couple who found the body because I think they left the village years ago," Stella said.

"What was their surname, Stella?" asked Ruth.

"It was Harrison. Don't you remember them Ruth? They were newlyweds who had been in the village only a few months, but soon after their gruesome find, they moved away. I think they went to one of the villages outside of York."

"No, I never met them. Remember George and I were in Hong Kong at the time."

Penny taking the lead once again, said, "Now is there anyone else that we've missed out? If not, we can begin to plan who will interview whom."

Cathy had one more idea. "How about we try to find the Yorkshire Post reporter who worked on the story at the time?"

"That's a good idea Cathy. Yes, let's try to track him down too," Sui Ling responded.

"Okay, let's now plan who will do the actual interviews," said Penny.

Cathy was quick to respond, "I'd like to interview Arthur Fisher."

"Okay, but not alone," responded Ruth. "Remember we must interview in twos."

Penny volunteered, "I'll go with her."

Ruth was the next to express a preference. "As I've already said, I'd like to meet with Gemma's parents. I'm sure I can do a better job than I did with Charlie's mother and father now that I realise their wounds are likely to be easily opened. Would anyone like to go with me?"

"I'll go with you," said Stella, "Who knows, we might even be able to get Peter to leave chambers for a short time to treat us to lunch."

Sui Ling said, "I'd like to visit Charlie's parents to see if I can get them onside in helping me to interview Charlie. I will present it as wanting to help clear his name once and for all, which of course, we'll do if he's not the guilty one."

Penny volunteered to accompany Sui Ling and followed up by saying, "I think it's important to schedule an interview with the ex-boyfriend as Cathy mentioned because, like Charlie and Arthur, he was a suspect for a time. Who'd be interested in that task?"

Ruth said she would do it when no-one else offered and then Penny volunteered to join her for that interview.

"Sui Ling, why don't you and I interview Pamela and Frank," said Stella. "I'm in need of a haircut and you could just accompany me unless you want to make an appointment too, and afterwards, we could have a drink at the White Hart. We'd be able to kill two birds with one stone so to speak because we'd be creating perfect opportunities to ask questions both at the hairdressers and in the pub."

"That's sounds great. Yes, I'm up for that. Now, I have dim sum ready to serve, so why don't we take a break, eat and then play a little Mahjong."

The conversation flowed as they all shared news of their family members while enjoying typical dim sum fare. There was char sui bao, steamed buns stuffed with barbecued pork, har gau, translucent shrimp dumplings and shu mai, steamed dumplings shaped like a basket with shrimp and pork filling. Sui Ling also offered a choice of green or jasmine tea.

So, engrossed had they become in planning their investigation that they'd almost forgotten this was a celebration for Penny and Cathy, but Sui Ling was not one to forget and, as soon as the dim sum dishes were cleared, she walked in with candles ablaze on the cake. Taking this as their cue, they all sang 'Happy Birthday' before Cathy and Penny blew out the candles together. After enjoying the cake, they headed to the Mahjong table for their very first game of the year.

"I thought we'd play the Western game today," Sui Ling told everyone. "Cathy, I know you still need a little help when we play this version, but if you sit and start to play, as soon as I've popped the dishes into the dishwasher, I'll come and help you to figure out some good hands to work towards,"

Before long, the sparrows were twittering and the ladies were feeling the excitement of being back at the Mahjong table once again.

"Oh, I definitely need your help Sui Ling; I've no idea what to do with these tiles," said Cathy.

"I'm coming; just give me a minute," Sui Ling replied, and soon all five were sitting together engrossed in working towards four very different hands.

Around and around the moves went, but no one was as excited as Ruth when she said she was fishing, but this was not just because she was close to winning, but because of the hand that she was attempting to complete. She couldn't wait to show everyone. Stella called out 'fishing' next and she was followed soon after by Penny, but still no-one was as eager to win as Ruth. Three more rounds passed and then Ruth picked up the very tile she wanted and whooped with joy as she called out 'Mahjong'.

"Look at this wonderful hand," she said as she laid down a 1, 8, 4 and 2 of circles and a 1, 9, 9 and 7 of bamboos along with a Pung of East Winds and another of West Winds. "I've never managed this hand before. It's called 'Hong Kong' and I'm thrilled to get it as Hong Kong is where I first learned to play Mahjong and it's where I first tasted dim sum. How fitting that here we are having dim sum today."

"Oh, that's wonderful, I never even knew that hand existed," said Sui Ling.

"Well, it's relatively new, of course, because the circles read 1842, the year that Hong Kong became a British Colony and the bamboos read 1997, which is when the territory was handed back to the Chinese and, of course, the winds reflect the combination of East and West," explained Ruth.

"It's a super hand. How much is he worth?" asked Stella.

"Well, if we were playing for money, then it would be worth double the limit because not only is it difficult to achieve in itself, but it's a concealed hand too, so every tile must be picked up from the wall rather than from discarded tiles, except for the last one, of course."

"Wonderful! I'll remember that one," added Sui Ling. "I think it will be quite easy to remember even if hard to achieve. Okay, let's play on and, Cathy, I'm going to sit with you again, but I will only help if you look to be struggling."

They played on for two more hours taking it in turns to sit out games before Sui Ling invited them to stop for tea and Chinese sweet treats. She also produced a bottle of sparkling wine for the birthday toast.

"Oh, these are delicious," said Penny. "What are they?"

"I'm glad you like them," Sui Ling replied. "They're my favourite too. They're called 'nian gao' and they're actually one of the most popular Chinese desserts. They're glutinous brown sugar cake wrapped in pastry and deep fried. Probably not the healthiest of foods," she laughed, "but oh so yummy!"

Stella agreed. "I think they're delicious too. Actually, I'm planning a little surprise for Peter's birthday on Valentine's Day. You must teach me how to make them so that I can make some for him. Oh, and you must all attend because you're the only guests I'm inviting. He usually likes a big gathering, but I just can't handle organising one right now because he's been a little strange and distant of late. I should say more than usual really because you all know we don't have the easiest of relationships so going all out on Valentine's Day seems a little inappropriate. Besides, it's not a big birthday; he'll be fifty-nine."

"We'll definitely be there," said Ruth. "Can I help you with anything at all? Actually, I'm sure everyone would like to help. Why don't we all bring a dish along and have a potluck dinner. In fact, if we want to really make it potluck, we could not say what we're bringing and just find out on the night," continued Ruth wryly.

"I'd love that and could certainly cope with five desserts being served. I love the Norwegian Christmas celebration where only sweet treats are served, but I think we need to be a more predictable for Peter; a table full of desserts or a table full of lasagnes would tax his sense of humour to the limit these days!"

Sui Ling offered to provide a dish of nian gao and one by one they suggested dishes that they might bring, so it wasn't long before the menu was set.

"I could organise a Valentine's 'Mr. and Mrs.' game for us to play if you think he'd like that," offered Cathy.

Stella laughed out loud. "That sounds like fun, but we'd probably lose right now. Maybe we should play a game where he has at least a chance of winning on his birthday. He quite likes 'Trivial Pursuit' and 'Charades.'"

"Oh, I bought the latest version of 'Trivial Pursuit' for Gregory at Christmas as he likes it too, so I can bring ours along," added Penny.

"That sounds like a plan. Thank you, and we have 'Charades' so I think we're set," replied Stella. "Now, I have a three o'clock appointment for a manicure, so I must say farewell."

"I think we're done for the day anyway," said Penny, "so let me just get this right. Ruth, you will go with Stella to see Gemma's parents and Cathy and Sui Ling, you're going to see Gemma's ex-boyfriend."

"No," interjected Sui Ling. "Penny is going with Ruth to talk to Gemma's ex. Don't worry, I've recorded everything we agreed and will email my notes to you all later today, so we just have to make our twosome arrangements to go and see whomever we're interviewing."

At that, farewells were said and arrangements for their next Mahjong game at Ruth's were made.

Chapter 9

The First Interviews

Penny was eager to start work which Cathy discovered when awoken from her slumber by the sound of a ping from her mobile.

"Hi, are you up for a drive to see Arthur Fisher today?" a message from Penny read.

"Sure," she messaged back. "What time?"

"Ready now if you are," responded Penny.

"Wow, you're up bright and early, I'm still in bed. Give me an hour," Cathy tapped into her phone.

"Okay. Pick you up at nine," Penny's next message read.

At nine on the dot, Cathy heard Penny's car arriving and she headed out of the door greeting Penny with, "Aren't you the early bird!"

"Well, you know what they say, 'The early bird catches the worm'," she chuckled. "Let's get our worm caught!"

Half an hour later, Penny drew the car to a stop right outside Arthur Fisher's little cottage and the two of them headed to the front door. Knock, knock, knock Cathy rapped on the door using the old rusty door knocker. Silence. She knocked again, but still no one answered and nothing could be heard from inside.

"Let's take a look through the windows," Penny suggested.

Together, the two of them, carefully avoiding the overgrown bramble, headed towards the front window that didn't have curtains closed and, somewhat gingerly, peered in under cupped hands. It was dark inside and there were no signs of life. They then headed to the back of the cottage and looked in through the kitchen window. The place was untidy and there were some unwashed dishes in the sink, but not a sign of life.

"Well, that was a waste of time," said Penny. "When will you be free to come again?"

"Most days are okay for me," Cathy said, "but we don't want another wasted journey, so let me try to find out if he has a landline or a mobile to call him on before heading out here again."

"Good idea, we should have tried doing that first, but I was just so eager to get going. Who's next on your list to interview?" Penny asked Cathy.

"I've got to try and find the Harrisons, the young couple who identified Arthur as the man they saw in the woods shortly before their dog found Gemma's body. What about you?" asked Cathy.

"I've got to interview Charlie's parents with Sui Ling. I tell you what, I'll ask Sui Ling if she can find out from Frank Cousins if he has a number for Arthur because Frank seems to know everybody and everything, and she and Stella are planning to interview him."

"Okay, but I'll still do some research to see what I can find out from directory enquiries and the electoral roll because I've got to check both to try and locate the Harrisons," Cathy replied.

On their way home, Cathy asked Penny to drop her off in the village because she had a few things to do before heading home. Penny obliged and as soon as she'd bid farewell to Cathy, she called Sui Ling to arrange their get together and they agreed to meet at the village coffee shop at ten thirty the next morning.

Meanwhile, Stella and Ruth were also making arrangements to begin their first task of interviewing Gemma's parents in Leeds.

"Hi, Stella. The Davies' are still living at the same address as they did when their daughter was murdered and I have their telephone number, so I'm planning to call them today, but just want to know when you'd be free to visit them?"

"I'm hosting a dinner on Friday for Peter's colleagues, so that's out. Tomorrow would be good, but preferably early next week either Monday or Wednesday because I still have to pick some things up for the dinner."

Ruth replied, "I know we don't want this to take from our family time, but what about Saturday if they prefer us to visit at the weekend?"

"No problem, you know Peter," said Stella. "I'll probably be a workaholic's widow at the weekend anyway, so I can be free on Saturday or Sunday."

"Well, Sundays are never good for me," said Ruth, "because we have church commitments in the morning and often get together with John and Becky later in the day, but I'm sure George will be all right with me going on Saturday if that's our only option. To be honest, he might appreciate a day to himself on the golf course. Anyway, I'll get back to you after I've spoken with them."

"Hello, is that Mrs. Davies?" Ruth asked in a kindly voice.

"Yes, it is," the voice at the other end of the telephone replied.

"I'm sorry to disturb you. My name is Ruth Cromwell and I live in Hazelby and, just recently, a small group of friends and I expressed great sadness when we discovered that your daughter, Gemma, never received justice. We've actually committed ourselves to going over events with fresh eyes in the hope of shedding light that will help to solve the case. I'm the wife of a police officer and I understand it's pretty much a cold case now, but we do want to re-investigate because something must have been missed in the initial investigation. I'm a mother myself and I can only imagine the heartache you've experienced and, if we can do anything to help at this stage to bring closure for all concerned, especially for you, we want to do it. I'd really like to talk to you and your husband if you can bring yourselves to going over the events once again. I'd be happy to drive over to meet with you both, so you could talk in the comfort of your own home."

"I appreciate your desire to help, Mrs. Cromwell, but this is something I would need to discuss with my husband first, so can I please call you back when I've had a chance to talk to him?"

"Of course!" Ruth replied. She then gave Mrs. Davies her number and said she would look forward to hearing from her.

The following day, Ruth received the promised call.

"Harold has agreed to meet with you. As he said, what harm can it do? To tell you the truth, we still feel the loss of Gemma every single day and anything that might serve to bring her killer to justice can only be a good thing as far as we're concerned."

Ruth replied, "Thank you. I'd also like to bring a member of the group that I'm working with too, if that's all right. Of course, we'll come at a time that's best for the two of you. We could actually come tomorrow or Saturday or one day next week if you prefer."

I think it would be better if you came next week to give us a little time to prepare ourselves. We're always home on Mondays so if you want to come next Monday that would be fine with us and you can choose your own time to visit."

"That's perfect," responded Ruth. "How about we come at two o'clock?"

"Yes, that's fine," said Mrs. Davies.

By ten forty-five the next morning, Penny and Sui Ling were already deep in discussion in the village coffee shop with steaming hot lattes in hand.

"I don't think that we should turn up on the Statham's doorstep as a twosome," said Sui Ling, "It could be too daunting and make them feel threatened in some way. I believe it would be better if just one of us goes to prepare the way, but we should go together to see Charlie if he agrees to see us."

"Yes, that sounds good," replied Penny. "I do know that Mrs. Statham was very upset when Ruth mentioned Charlie before Christmas. Do you want to go or shall I? I'm happy to go but tend to think that you'd be the best one because at least you know Charlie."

"Yes, I do know him, but I'm not sure I'm the best because I'm a bit 'John Blunt' or so I'm told. To be honest, Ruth would be great, but this is down to the two of us and I think you have a lovely way with people. It really doesn't matter that you don't know him. In fact, it may be an advantage as they will, hopefully, realise you have no preconceived ideas about their son," said Sui Ling.

"Well, there's no time like the present. I'll stroll over to see if they're home as soon as I've finished my coffee." In less than half an hour, Penny was standing outside the front door of a little terraced house not far from the coffee shop.

After just one knock, she found herself face-to-face with Mr. Statham and was quick to introduce herself.

"Mr. Statham, you may remember me. I'm Penny McKenzie. I live in Little Hazelby, but I'm often here in the village and I know our paths have crossed from time to time even though we've never been formally introduced."

"Yes, I know who you are. What can I do for you?" he cautiously replied.

"I'd really like to discuss something personal with you and Mrs. Statham that I'm hoping will be a big help to the two of you and to Charlie too. Could I please come in?"

He opened the door wide without another word and Penny stepped inside at the same time as he called out to his wife. "Doris, someone's here to see us."

Mrs. Statham made an appearance at the end of the hallway and invited Penny to come through to the kitchen where she'd obviously been busy peeling vegetables. Mr. Statham pulled out a chair for Penny to sit down and she very soon found herself facing the two of them sitting at the other side of the table.

"I'm sorry to barge in unannounced, but I would really like your help because with a few friends, I'm trying to get to the bottom of the Gemma Davies case. I understand that this is still a painful topic for you because of the way that Charlie was treated, but we're not against him. Quite the reverse, because we want to investigate the case in the hope of finding something that was missed and that could lead to Charlie being totally exonerated instead of still being thought to be guilty by some of the villagers."

"He's not guilty!" Mrs. Statham barked. "He would never hurt a fly. I wish I'd never heard of the name Gemma Davies, for that's when everything started to go wrong for Charlie."

"I understand and would love to help you prove that because until the real murderer is found, Charlie will always be implicated. We both know that there are those who say that insufficient evidence against him does not mean he's innocent."

By this time, Mrs. Statham was in tears and her husband was trying to console her.

"Doris, this could be the very thing we've been hoping for, a chance to clear Charlie's name once and for all."

"I would need to talk to Charlie himself," said Penny, "but, of course, with the two of you present."

"We can't speak for Charlie," said Mr. Statham, "but I will certainly ask him and encourage him to talk to you because anything that will clear his name would be welcome. He's been living under a cloud ever since the day he was taken in for questioning and, to be honest, no one else has ever offered any help."

"Thank you. Here's my number," said Penny as she passed a piece of paper across the table. "Actually, I'd like my friend Sui Ling to join us too. I'm sure you know her; her husband owns the Green Dragon. So, please, could you ask Charlie if he would meet with us both?" Penny ended the conversation by saying, "Now, I won't take up any more of your time and I look forward to hearing from you and meeting with Charlie when it's convenient."

Mr. Statham saw Penny to the door, but just before closing it, he said "Thank you" with real appreciation in his voice.

The weekend passed uneventfully, but on Monday morning Ruth and Stella set about tasks that would free them up for the rest of the day. Ruth prepared dinner in advance as she knew she'd be late home and Stella visited the tied cottage where her elderly housekeeper and gardener lived to check up on Eric's health and to plan the week's work with Brenda.

At one o'clock, Ruth picked up Stella and they hit the road. Once in Leeds, Stella put the Davies' address into the GPS which then led them straight to their home where Ruth and Stella found themselves warmly welcomed by Mrs. Davies.

"Please come through. I have a pot of tea and some home-made scones in case you're feeling a little peckish after your drive."

Ruth thanked her and introduced both herself and Stella before the four of them sat down together in the living room.

"It's very kind of you to see us both Mr. and Mrs. Davies. I realise this is not easy for you," said Ruth.

"Please call us Joan and Harold," Mrs. Davies replied. "You're right, it's not easy, but neither is living with the pain that has never gone away. I'm not sure it ever will but getting to the bottom of what happened and why would surely help. Please just ask us any questions you have and we'll try our best to answer."

"Well, I think it would be nice for us just to get to know one another first, so let me tell you a little about us. Stella, and I both live in Hazelby, a village just ten miles from where Gemma was found, and we play Mahjong together with three other ladies. Your daughter's case came up in conversation and we all felt so sad that it had never been resolved and before we knew it, we were all committed to doing our best to trace over the steps to see if we could find anything that had been missed in the official investigation. My husband, George, is with the police force and Stella's husband, Peter, is a barrister, so both will be a big help to us."

"We're happy to know you all want to help, aren't we, Harold?" Joan responded.

"Yes," Harold replied. "Although I don't know what we can tell you that's not been said to the police already."

"Maybe, you could tell us a little about yourselves and Gemma's life before she was so cruelly taken," suggested Stella.

"Well, we're both retired now, but Harold was a bus driver for most of his working life and I was a clerk in the local Council office," said Joan. "We've actually lived in this house since the day we got married and Gemma was born here in the front bedroom. She was our only child and was a good girl but, in her teenage years, she became a little rebellious and, although she was clever enough to have taken her A-levels, she left school at sixteen and by the time she was eighteen she'd already moved into a flat with her best friend, Sharon, from school. They were like sisters."

As she finished speaking, Stella's phone rang and she apologised and excused herself as she stepped out into the hall to answer it. Joan took the opportunity to refresh the teapot and returned from the kitchen at the very same time as Stella came back into the room, ashen faced.

"Whatever is wrong, Stella?" asked Ruth.

"That was a call from the police. Peter's been in an accident and has been taken to the Infirmary. I must go!"

"Of course," said Ruth. "I'll drive you." Turning to Joan and Harold she said, "I'm so sorry, but I know you will understand we need to leave immediately. I will be in touch again as soon as possible."

"Yes, of course, you must go. Please don't worry about us. We're just so sorry this has happened and do hope that all will be well with your husband, Stella."

"Thank you," Stella said as she and Ruth left the house in a hurry.

As they drove towards the hospital passing estate after estate, each with almost identical homes and then on through an industrial estate the drabness of the environment did nothing to lift their spirits. Rather, it seemed to intensify the depressive air that had descended upon them both following the phone call.

"What did they say exactly," asked Ruth?

Almost robotically, Stella answered, "They just told me that he's been in a car accident and to get to the hospital as quickly as possible."

Talking seemed to open her up and she began to weep silently and shared her fears. "It sounds so serious, Ruth. I don't know what I'm going to find or do."

"I'll be with you every step of the way, Stella, just try your best not to worry before we find out what's what."

Chapter 10

The Suspect

When they arrived at the hospital, Stella expected to be able to see Peter straight away, but she was told he was in theatre.

"Go and grab a couple of seats over by the window," said Ruth, "while I buy some hot drinks."

Still somewhat on auto pilot, Stella complied.

"Here's a nice cup of strong tea. I probably won't be able to go in to see Peter with you when he gets out of theatre, but I won't leave until you're ready to go home too, so don't worry about a thing," Ruth said reassuringly. "Now, do you want me to ring Marcus for you or do you want to leave that call for a while?"

"I don't know. What do you think?" Stella replied.

"Well, it's probably best to wait until you've had a chance to talk to the doctor," suggested Ruth, "because we don't really have anything to tell him yet."

Just as she'd finished speaking, she saw a young police officer making his way towards them.

"Mrs. Benchley-Smythe," he said, "I was one of the officers on the scene after your husband's accident. If you feel up to talking, I'd like to tell you what I know and answer any questions you have if I can."

"Yes, I want to know what happened. I have no idea," Stella replied.

"Well, my partner and I were called to an accident on the A64. Your husband was unconscious in his car when we arrived. Actually, he's very lucky to be alive because the car's a write-off and he had to be cut out. He took a direct hit from a van that swerved across from the opposite side of the road. He must have seen the van coming because he had the presence of mind to swerve himself and so avoid a head-on collision, but the van did hit his car hard enough to turn it over. The eye-witnesses all agree that the fault lies with the van driver, but, like your husband, he's in no fit state to be interviewed yet."

"Is Peter going to be all right?"

"I'm no medic so I'll leave the doctor to speak to you about his medical condition, but, if you have any questions about the crash, I might be able to answer those."

"No, I just want to see my husband," Stella responded.

It was another forty-five minutes before a nurse came over to tell Stella that she could now see Peter.

"What about my friend, can she come with me?" Stella asked the nurse.

"No, I'm sorry, but, at this stage, one visitor in the room is enough."

"Go ahead, Stella," urged Ruth. "I'll wait here and be ready to drive you home later."

Stella was shocked to see Peter wired up to machines with a cannula inserted into the back of his left hand and lying motionless on the bed. His normally imposing figure appeared to have shrunk and his face was so swollen that he was hardly recognisable. She went straight to his bedside and touched his right hand gently and, in a soft voice said, "Peter, it's me, Stella. Can you hear me?"

He didn't respond and she then felt someone touch her arm. Looking up, she saw a doctor, who just as gently as she had spoken to Peter, said, "I'm sorry, but he can't hear you at the moment. He's in a medically induced coma because he has some swelling on the brain. As you can see, one side of his face took a heavy blow and for the time being we want to give his brain a rest. This is normal procedure in such circumstances so please don't be too alarmed."

"Is he going to be all right?" she asked.

"Well, both of his legs are broken and he has several broken ribs, but fortunately none of them pierced his lungs. We've already operated and set the bones in his legs and there's no reason why he shouldn't be able to walk again in time. As for his head injuries, we just need to wait and see, but I'm hopeful as I've seen people recover from worse. For now, he'll just need careful monitoring. We're going to keep him in the coma for a few days, at least until the swelling subsides, so I suggest you go home and get some rest yourself and then come back to see him tomorrow."

"No, I'm not going to leave him. Can I please stay in the room with him?"

"Well, you can, but you won't be very comfortable as we don't have any guest beds here. There's only a chair for you to sleep on, but, if you insist, I can ask a nurse to bring a blanket for you in case it turns cold in the night."

"Yes, yes, I'll be fine. Thank you. I'll just let my friend know that I'm staying here so that she can go home," and with that both Stella and the doctor left the room.

"Ruth, I'm going to stay with Peter overnight, so please don't feel you need to stay any longer."

"How is he?" Ruth asked.

Stella related what she'd been told and Ruth left, but not before assuring Stella that she could ring her at any time if she needed any help whatsoever.

The next morning, once everyone had arrived at Ruth's for their Mahjong session, she filled them in on why Stella was absent. Understandably, no one felt much like playing, so they simply updated each other on the progress they'd made so far and talked about the next steps each of them intended to take.

Cathy reported that her investigations had drawn a blank regarding a telephone number for Arthur Fisher, so Penny said, "Well, as we're not going to be playing today, maybe the two of us can take another drive up there to see if we can catch him at home this time.

"Yes, let's," Cathy responded, "but I did manage to have some success in my telephone number hunt because I have numbers for a couple of Tony Stapleford's in Leeds. You remember, Gemma's ex-boyfriend. Shall I give you the numbers, Ruth, or will you be calling Penny?"

"I'm happy to make calls, Penny, seeing that you and Cathy are heading straight up to Bentham Woods. I actually need to call Gemma's parents, too, and let them know what happened with Stella as we left in such a hurry yesterday. In fact, as Stella is not going to be in any fit state to work on the investigation for a while, would you be able to come with me next time, Sui Ling?"

"No problem. Just let me know when because I'm also slated to visit Charlie with Penny if we get the go-ahead from his parents."

"Okay, I'll give them a call and, if they are willing, I'll arrange a visit as soon as possible," said Ruth. "Would you be free tomorrow if I can arrange it?"

"Yes, no problem, but, if you hear from the Statham's today, Penny, don't fix up a trip for us tomorrow. Thursday afternoon or anytime on Friday would work."

"Got it," replied Penny.

Very soon, they were all saying farewell once again, but not before setting up a WhatsApp group especially for the investigation to keep each other up to date as it was becoming obvious that they needed to keep in close contact and not rely solely upon their weekly meetings.

Once everyone had left, Ruth called Gemma's parents, but unfortunately, they were not available the following day, so she arranged to visit on Friday morning. She then quickly messaged the group so that Penny and Sui Ling would know of this change of plan.

As Cathy and Penny drew up outside Arthur Fisher's home, it looked as eerily vacant as it did the first time they'd visited. They knocked and peered through the windows as they did before and could see that the dishes were still unwashed and nothing had been moved.

"He's obviously away somewhere, but I don't know how we can find out when he will be back. It's not as if he has any neighbours we can ask, so I guess we're just going to have to keep popping back until he returns," said Penny.

"I wonder whether Frank at the White Hart would know anything," replied Cathy. "Who was scheduled to visit him?"

"Stella was for sure and I think Sui Ling was going with her, but we could offer to go instead. What do you think?"

"Yes, Sui Ling may be glad of us doing that now she's going with Ruth to Leeds."

Within half an hour, they were ordering drinks at the bar of the White Hart and chatting with the landlord. After a few pleasantries, Penny got straight to the point.

"Frank, how well do you know Arthur Fisher, the old man who lives up by Bentham Woods, because we've stopped by there a couple of times and there's no sign of life?"

"What would you two be wanting with old Arthur?"

"We're just interested in the murder that took place up there and wanted to ask him a few questions."

"Why are you interested in that case?"

"Well, it's a cold case that took place on our doorstep and we're wondering if there was anything missed at the time that we could maybe bring to light. We just want to talk to everyone who was involved."

"Your talk with Arthur might have to wait a while as he's in and out of hospital these days. He used to pop in here for a drink when he came down for supplies, but not so often since being diagnosed with cancer."

"Oh, that's sad. Yes, perhaps he's in hospital as it doesn't look as if he's been home for a while. Do you have a number for him?" asked Cathy.

"I don't and to be honest, I can't imagine he's the mobile phone type. I know he has a sister in York who keeps an eye on him, but I don't have a number for her either, so I think you'll just have to keep popping up there until you find him in."

As their conversation with Frank was ending, another was beginning, but across the village in Ruth's cottage.

"Hello, could I speak to Tony Stapleford please?"

"Yes, speaking. Who is this?"

"I'm sorry, you don't know me, but my name is Ruth Cromwell, and I'm trying to contact people who knew Gemma Davies twenty years or more ago?" Is that name familiar to you?"

"No, I'm sorry, the name doesn't ring a bell, but then I've only lived in this area for the past four years."

"Oh, I see. I'm so sorry to have troubled you," Ruth said.

"No problem; I hope you find who you're looking for."

Ruth thanked him before ending the call and she then dialled the second number.

"Yes," the voice at the other end of the phone said. "Who is this?"

Ruth's words followed the same pattern as in the previous call, but her reception was not as gracious after she said who she was and why she was calling.

"Yes, it is, but I've no interest in talking to you. I had nothing to do with her murder and the police know that which is why I was never charged."

"I'm not suggesting for one minute that you did Mr. Stapleford; in fact, just the opposite, but, as she was a friend of yours, I'm sure you'd like to see whoever was responsible caught."

"What's it got to do with you anyway?" he replied.

"Well, I live in the area where she was found and I belong to a group who would like to see justice being served for everybody's sake, including yours, because until it's known who committed that horrendous act, suspicion will always hang over your head and others who were in your situation. You know how people like to say, 'there's no smoke without fire'. I don't actually subscribe to that view myself, but many do. I believe that if we can find clues that lead to the killer, no one will ever question your involvement again."

At this, his tone changed and he said, "Okay, what do you want to know?"

"Well, would it be possible for me and a friend to come and see you?"

"No, please ask what you want to know. I prefer to get this over and done with now and I don't want to involve my wife and children in this case."

"I understand. I guess, I'd just like to know a little bit more about your relationship with Gemma. I believe you'd already broken up by the time she was murdered. How did that happen?"

"Oh, it was always an on-off relationship. We were young and both of us kept straying so I guess we were never meant to be anyway."

"Did you know any of the other men in her life?"

"Sure, every time we got back together, we came clean with each other, but I didn't know anyone personally. She met one or two through work; for example, she worked up at the student university bar three evenings a week at one time and dated one or two students during a couple of our early break ups. There was one guy that she talked a lot about at the time. He was a medical student, but I can't remember his name, although I think it began with a 'G' maybe Graham or Greg; I'm just not sure. There were others too, but, once she gave up her job there, she found guys to date from the bar she was working in downtown. I remember one guy's name, Simon, because he was the son of a big noise. His dad owned Carson's Construction. I think he still does."

"So, when did you finally break up?"

"At least a year before she was found dead, so I don't know why I was ever a suspect."

"I understand. Is there anything else that you can tell me, particularly that didn't come out at the time, but now, in hindsight, you think might help shed some light in the darkness?"

"Not that I can think of right now."

"Okay, but would you call me if anything at all occurs to you? I'll leave you my number."

"Yes, I will, but no need to give me your number, it's showing up here on my phone."

"Thank you. Would you also be all right with me calling you again if I need to follow up?"

"No problem. Anything that might help to clear my name of the slightest suspicion is fine by me."

"Thanks again. I will keep you posted on how things go."

Ruth made another call. "Hi Penny, I've just been speaking with Gemma's ex and we don't need to visit. He didn't want to meet, but he was happy to talk over the phone. It seems our Gemma was something of a serial dater. There may be many leads to follow, but he did give me a couple of vague names and one of a young man who should be easy to find. Let me know when you're free to come over and I'll fill you in so that we can decide together whether we need to talk to him again or just report back to everyone on Tuesday."

"That's good news in that it saves us a trip. How does tomorrow sound? I've not heard back from the Statham's yet, so I'm free and if they do call, I'll work around our meeting. Shall I come around ten in the morning?"

"Perfect. I'll see you then."

At ten the next morning, Penny drove up to Ruth's, excited that things were at last beginning to move.

"Hi Ruth, how are you? I've brought a couple of bran muffins with me."

"Oh, lovely, they're still warm," Ruth said as she took the brown bag from Penny.

"Let me put the kettle on and I'll fill you in."

One hour later, Penny left Ruth's, but her excitement had turned into chilling fear. It had started to well up inside her the minute she'd heard about Gemma being involved with a medical student and the possible name of Greg being connected. As she drove home, her mind whirled. Surely this couldn't be Gregory. Was he ever known as Greg? She'd never called him Greg and no one she knew ever did. No, of course it couldn't be him. Oh, but he was definitely a medical student at Leeds University until the year before Gemma's death, so he could have known her. No, if he'd known this girl, he would have said. Oh, but he really was against me getting involved in this case. Could that be because he knew her? No, he was just concerned for my safety. Is that the truth or is there a more sinister reason? Could he be the murderer? Of course not! Questions and doubts continued to fill her mind for the rest of the drive home despite her trying her best to eliminate them.

Chapter 11

The Questions

By the time Gregory returned from the hospital that evening, Penny had almost convinced herself that the Greg who'd been briefly named in connection with Gemma Davies was not her Gregory. Besides, the ex-boyfriend wasn't even sure himself that the medical student was called Greg. He could just as easily have been called Graham or some other name beginning with a 'G'; nevertheless, she knew she wouldn't rest until she knew for sure.

After dinner, when Gregory brought them a glass of wine each and they sat in front of the open fire, she broached the subject with him in a roundabout way. She wanted to get to the truth without him becoming defensive or feeling attacked.

"Gregory, I'm puzzled about why you are so against me getting involved in the Gemma Davies case. You don't usually object or interfere with anything I do."

"I've already told you, it's a foolhardy plan. I think there are far better ways to spend your time."

"What's so foolhardy about it?"

"Are you serious? You really don't see the dangers involved in such a venture?"

"Of course, there are risks, but we're minimising them as none of us will go anywhere alone. By the way, do you know what I found out today? Gemma Davies actually worked at the university bar when you were a student there."

Penny watched his reaction intently and she was sure she detected a slight ruffle in his normally cool, calm demeanour. Without giving him time to answer, she continued.

"Did you go in the bar much in those days?"

"No more nor less than any other student. Well, perhaps a little more as I was in the wine club remember."

"So, did you ever come across this girl because her ex-boyfriend told Ruth that she'd had a fling with a medical student whose name began with a 'G'. He thought it was either Graham or Greg. Did they call you Greg in those days? There can't be many Greg's who were medical students at the time, so I'm going to ask you a question and I want a straight answer. Was it you?"

Gregory almost choked on his drink and began coughing. He didn't need to say another word because his reaction and face said it all. The one thing she felt sure about with Gregory is that he was no liar; in fact, she really believed that he wouldn't be able to lie, even to save his own life.

"So, you really are the mysterious Greg! It's no wonder you didn't want me digging into this case."

"All right, yes I did know her, but you've got to believe me when I say that I had nothing to do with her death."

"Well, why didn't you come clean at the time when the police were asking questions?"

"They never actually questioned me. I don't know why, but I guess as someone who'd had a fling with her long before she was murdered, they were not interested in me or perhaps my name just never came up. I've no idea; maybe they already had their suspects, but I was hardly going to volunteer myself as a possible suspect was I!"

"But why didn't you at least come clean with me at Christmas when I told you about the case?"

"For this very reason. Imagine, if this discussion had taken place when the boys were here!"

"So why didn't you bring it up after they left?"

"I didn't think there was any point in raking up the past."

Her voice now raised, Penny almost shouted, "What! You knew we are going to dig. Why would you let me walk into the most embarrassing trap I could imagine and in front of my friends?"

"Just a minute, I'm the one who tried to stop you, remember."

At this, her resolve to keep calm deserted her and she yelled, "Not with the truth you didn't. For all I know, you could be her murderer!"

"Don't be stupid. I took an oath to save lives not to end them," he threw back at her. "When all is said and done, all I'm guilty of is not coming clean about having had a fling with her that was long before I met you and long before she was murdered."

Penny knew he was telling the truth, but she was now thinking about whether this was something she should divulge to the group or keep to herself.

"What on earth am I going to tell Ruth and the rest of the group?" she asked Gregory.

"Why do you have to tell them anything?"

"Well, what happens if they decide to search for this unknown Graham or Greg and end up discovering it's you?"

"Look, let's face that if it happens."

"But if I don't say anything and then they find out it's you, what are they going to think? No, I'm going to tell them the truth, so you'd better start talking and tell me the whole story. I want to know everything about your relationship with her from beginning to end."

Gregory felt he had little choice but to do this Penny's way and the two of them talked until they were exhausted from the emotional strain of the whole affair.

On Friday, Ruth and Sui Ling headed to Leeds as planned to take up where Ruth and Stella had left off. Harold and Joan seemed happy to see them and continued talking enthusiastically, revealing their deep love for Gemma. They shared how pleased they'd been when she'd started to train as a beautician. It was obvious that they didn't like the bar life she'd been leading. Ruth and Sui Ling listened sympathetically and from time to time, asked questions. They were particularly interested in hearing more about her life with Sharon.

"Do you know what happened to Sharon?" Sui Ling enquired.

"Oh, yes, she's married now and has become like a daughter to us. In fact, after she lost her own mother, I became a surrogate grandma to her children. They love Harold too, especially her son, Craig, as they both support Leeds United and Harold occasionally takes him to matches."

"Do you think she would mind talking to us?" asked Ruth.

Joan was quick to reply. "I'm sure she'd be more than happy to meet you as she's never got over losing her best friend. Our love for Gemma is something that has kept us close over the years and I know she too, would love to see justice done. I can actually ring her now to ask if her, if you'd like me to do so."

"Yes, please do. Does she live nearby?" asked Ruth.

"Not too far, just a fifteen-minute drive away. Would you like to see her today if she's free?"

"Yes, yes, that would be very helpful."

As Joan walked into the kitchen with teapot in hand, she was already calling Sharon and, by the time she returned with a fresh pot of tea and a plate of biscuits, a meeting had been arranged.

"Sharon can't come here as her daughter, Poppy, is unwell, but she would be more than happy for you both to go there to see her. I've told her that I'm going to give you another cup of tea and then send you on your way."

Back in Little Hazelby, Penny was feeling happier and more in control. She still didn't know whether to tell the girls about Gregory's connection with Gemma Davies or not, but she no longer had concerns about his possible involvement in the murder. What's more she'd just received a call from Mrs. Statham informing her that Charlie had agreed to talk. All that needed to be done now was to find a time that would work for all of them.

Cathy, on the other hand, was not finding her allotted task straightforward. Knowing that Stella would not be able to interview the hairdresser for some time, she had popped in to see Pamela herself in the hopes that she would be able to help her trace the Harrisons. All had seemed to be going well because Pamela had given Cathy an address but, failing to observe the rule of two because she didn't think there was any risk, she had gone to visit them alone. However, that's where she had hit a brick wall in her investigation. She had discovered that they were no longer at the address Pamela had given her. The new residents told her they'd only been in the house for a year and all they could tell her was that the previous owners were not called Harrison. They did, however, give her the name of the Estate Agent who'd listed the house and brokered their purchase. Cathy hoped it would turn into a good lead, but she had no time to visit their offices and so headed back home planning to call the agent later.

In Leeds Infirmary, Stella was in a meeting of her own. She was with Peter's consultant who had just told her that he'd seen sufficient progress to bring Peter out of the coma and that this would be done the following day. Unfortunately, he couldn't assure her that all would be well. All he could say was that once conscious, they'd be able to assess his condition more accurately. As soon as the meeting was over, she rang Marcus to give him this news.

Also, in Leeds, Ruth and Sui Ling, following Harold's directions, found themselves at Sharon's door within an hour of her invitation.

"Please come in," said Sharon. "I'm sorry I couldn't come over to see you, but I'm so happy that at long last someone is taking an interest in the case. Living without Gemma in my life has been hard enough because we were like sisters and knowing that whoever murdered her is still walking the streets makes it even worse. I want to help you in any way that I can, so please ask me any questions you have because there has to be a clue to be found somewhere!"

Sharon shared details of their life together, their rebelliousness and the fun that they'd had as teens living in their own flat and Ruth and Sui Ling listened carefully, analysing every word as they looked for clues. Sharon's memories made her happy, that is until she began to share about their last evening together. She became emotional and found it much harder to talk. Ruth and Sui Ling took it in turns to gently ask her questions as they were particularly interested in hearing more about Gemma's secret lover who had been mentioned in the papers and who, according to Frank Cousins' theory, was the guilty party.

"What can you tell us about this man?" asked Ruth.

"To be honest, very little because this is one area of Gemma's life that she kept pretty much to herself. I know he was older than her and loaded and she told me he'd promised to leave his wife. When she found out she was pregnant, I know she was happy because she felt this would be the very thing that would prompt him to the point of leaving his wife. I actually think she was so eager to give him the news that she got up early to go and see him the next morning before I'd even got out of bed." Stifling tears, she said quietly, "I never saw her again!"

Ruth patted her arm and handed her a tissue before continuing. "Can you recall anything more that might help us to identify him because if we can discover who this mystery man is, we might be able to make some real headway?"

Composed once again, Sharon said, "Well, I think he insisted that Gemma not talk to anyone about their relationship because before he came on the scene, she would tell me everything. We both shared every detail of our love lives before then. Actually, it's a strange thing to silence someone if you truly love them, don't you think? Maybe he was really well-known and an affair could ruin his reputation. Who knows?"

"Do you know where he took her when they went out?" asked Sui Ling. "If we could identify a few of the places they frequented, we might be able to find some people who remember them and perhaps discover just who he was."

"I don't. Honestly, in the last year of her life, she was just so secretive. I got the feeling though that he never took her anywhere local. I think he had his own flat in some posh area, but, again, she was so closed when it came to their relationship that if he did, I wouldn't be able to tell you where."

They talked for another hour and by the time Ruth and Sui Ling left, they had a pretty good picture of who Gemma was, but, unfortunately, they were no further forward in discovering the identity of her secret lover.

That evening, WhatsApp messages flew back and forth as each of them shared brief updates on their activities agreeing to share full details at their next Mahjong session.

The next morning as Peter was being brought back to consciousness, with Stella by his side, Cathy was on the phone to the agent briefly explaining the reason for her call. He confirmed that he had indeed dealt with the Harrison's sale of the home some four years earlier and had contact details for them from that time. However, he refused to give them to Cathy saying that he'd be happy to do so if the Harrisons gave their permission and he promised to get back to her later.

"Peter, it's me," Stella said taking him by the hand. "I've been so worried about you. How are you feeling?"

Peter squeezed her hand, but, though his lips moved as if to speak, no sound came from them. She looked up at the doctor who assured her that his vital signs were all good and that she just needed to be patient a while longer. That afternoon, she was rewarded when he spoke his first words.

"I'm so sorry," he managed to say.

"Shhh," Stella replied. "It's okay, everything's going to be all right. Just concentrate on resting and getting strong again."

Again, he squeezed her hand before closing his eyes, but not before she saw tears welling up in them.

Cathy was at home when she received the expected call from the estate agent.

"Mrs. Skidmore? This is Jonathan Ford. We spoke this morning about the Harrisons. I'm so sorry, but Mr. Harrison has not given me permission to pass on his contact details. He did ask me to explain that the whole incident was so very traumatic for his wife that it led to her having a breakdown from which she has never fully recovered. He went on to say that she's remained very emotional and has been in and out of psychiatric hospitals ever since, and he just does not want her to have to re-visit that time, nor does he want to talk about it either. He added that he'd reported everything to the police at the time and has nothing more to add anyway."

"Thank you. I appreciate you trying," said Cathy before ending the call."

She then thought about the possibility of driving up to see if Arthur Fisher was home but reasoned that she wouldn't be able to speak with him alone if he was, so she dismissed that idea and began to focus upon her next task. This was to try and locate the Yorkshire Post reporter who'd covered the case. She busied herself doing what she could while awaiting news from everyone else.

Chapter 12

The Penny Drops

"Hi Sui Ling!" Penny's voice rang out. "It's so good that Charlie has agreed to talk. We just need to offer the Statham's a couple of days that would work for us to visit him. Which ones are best for you?"

"Monday works, but, if that's not possible, then Wednesday," replied Sui Ling.

"Okay, I'll call them and get back to you later when I know which day they prefer."

"Perfect!"

Penny immediately called the Statham's who agreed that Monday would be the best day for them but said they'd need to check with Charlie first. Feeling sure it would be okay, Mrs. Statham said she'd only call back if that was a problem. Penny, on the assumption that it would be okay, said she'd pick them up at ten o'clock so that they could all travel together in her car. She then WhatsApped Sui Ling to confirm the arrangement.

Sunday was a family day at home for everyone but Stella and Peter. However, thanks to a surprise visitor, it turned into a family day in the hospital too. Marcus popped his head around Peter's hospital door in the early afternoon with flowers for his mum and kind words for his dad, which, after their last parting, were welcome indeed.

"So good to see you, son," Peter said warmly.

"Marcus, why didn't you tell me you were coming?" Stella asked. "I could have picked you up at the airport."

"That's exactly why I didn't tell you. I figured you'd got enough on your plate without coming to pick me up. Taxis are ten a penny at the airport, so I really didn't need you to go to the trouble of coming for me."

"Oh, I'm so glad you're here. How long can you stay?"

"It's a flying visit I'm afraid as I need to be back for a meeting on Tuesday to discuss the details of my upcoming exhibition. I'm booked on a flight tomorrow afternoon, so short and sweet, but I just wanted to check on the 'old man' for myself."

"Not so much of the old," Peter said with a smile.

They all laughed and the cordial atmosphere continued, ensuring that their family day turned out to be as pleasant as their last meeting was ugly.

On Monday morning, as planned, Penny went to pick up Sui Ling.

"Good morning! This is going to be a good day. I can feel it in my bones," said Sui Ling as she got into Penny's car.

Penny laughed and said, "I hope you're right. It has the potential to be explosive if Charlie goes on the defensive."

"I agree. He's a bit of an unknown quantity, so I guess we'll just have to play it by ear and be careful to come across as supportive and non-judgmental."

Ten minutes later they picked up the Statham's and following Mr. Statham's directions, they soon found themselves leaving their pretty village with its stone-built homes and cosy atmosphere, behind. Once on the North Yorkshire moors, the grey tarmac roads simply merged into what was now the barren landscape of winter. The wind whistled as they drove across a flat expanse, which was in stark contrast to its summer vista when drivers would experience mile after mile of heather in bloom.

Eventually, Mr. Statham told Penny to leave the solitary road and she found herself driving along a gravel track, which soon led them downhill and into a desolate spot in the valley which couldn't be seen from the road above. In fact, all that could be seen was a small, run-down caravan by the side of a stream. This was Charlie's home.

Mrs. Statham was the first to get out of the car and she went immediately to the door of the caravan and began knocking.

"Charlie, it's me, mum. Please open the door. Dad's here and the two ladies who want to help clear your name are here too."

The man who appeared at the door did not resemble the photographs of the young man who'd effectively been chased out of his home almost twenty years ago. He was gaunt, dishevelled and a somewhat dirty looking individual who looked much older than his years. Without meeting their gaze, he stepped back to allow them to come in. There was little room inside the caravan, but it was so bitterly cold outside that all four of them quickly entered and squeezed around the little dining table that dropped down to become a bed. It was not much warmer inside the van, but at least they'd escaped the biting January wind. Charlie pulled up a folding chair, which had seen better days, and placed it at the end of the table, sitting on it without saying a word.

Mr. Statham was the first to speak. "How are you doing, son?" Without waiting for a response, he continued, "We've brought you some groceries that I'll get out of the boot for you before we leave."

Charlie just nodded and Mrs. Statham joined the one-sided conversation by asking, "How's your cough? Did the medication I brought you help at all?"

Again, Charlie nodded, but this time it was accompanied by an almost inaudible 'yes' and 'thanks' before he fell silent again.

Penny was the next to speak, but she didn't waste any time in getting to the point of the reason for their visit.

"Thank you for agreeing to talk to us about the Gemma Davies case, Charlie. May I call you Charlie?"

"Yes, that's fine," he responded clearly and, when he followed with the words, "I'm grateful for your interest in helping to clear my name because no one has ever shown any positive interest in me before now," both Sui Ling and Penny were stunned. This man, who just minutes ago had seemed as if he was going to be hard work, had come to life in a surprisingly articulate way.

"That's great. I'm Penny and this is my friend Sui Ling," she said. "If you'd be happy to share details of what happened from your perspective at that time, it will help us to get a broader picture, and if you wouldn't mind, we'd also like to ask questions as you talk if we have any."

Charlie nodded and then he talked, hardly pausing for breath.

"The first time I ever heard the girl's name was when the police took me down to the station for questioning. It was within hours of her body being found. I didn't even know there'd been a murder when they came to the house.

"I was questioned for hours. They kept asking me the same questions over and over again and, no matter how many times I told them I was innocent, they didn't seem to want to listen. It's only because they had absolutely no evidence linking me to her murder that they let me go.

"Still, mud sticks, you know, and from that day on, even though the police never charged me, I was treated like a pariah in the village. She lost her life, but, in a way, so did I. The treatment I received afterwards was so unbearable, I eventually had to get away.

"I thought I had friends in the village, but no-one offered me any support but my parents. I was essentially sent to Coventry and that was the easiest of the things I had to endure. When anyone did speak to me, it was only to hurl verbal abuse and, sometimes, I even suffered physical attacks too. I wasn't even safe in my own home; for example, one evening a brick was thrown through my living room window only narrowly missing my head.

"I always thought the rule of law meant innocent until proven guilty, but that's just a fallacy because, in my experience, you are guilty until proven innocent and punished too! When people decide for themselves you are guilty, their punishment is worse than any that could be handed out in a court. I think I'd have fared better going to prison than being driven into isolation. Frankly, I'd have been dead myself by now if it hadn't been for mum and dad."

Charlie just continued pouring it all out. It seemed that the floodgates had opened because he talked almost non-stop. He even admitted to his own criminal record and what he said some would call his perverted behaviour.

Sui Ling and Penny had no questions whatsoever. They listened to every word and felt this man's pain and that of his parents. They were filled with compassion for him and this strengthened their resolve to get to the bottom of this case if it was humanly possible. They shared their hearts for him with his parents on the drive home and Mrs. Statham was overcome with emotion. Finally, she thought, there was hope on the horizon for her family.

By the time Penny and Sui Ling arrived back in Little Hazelby, Cathy had come to another dead end. The Yorkshire Post reporter who had covered the case from beginning to end had passed away three years earlier, so all that remained were his written words in the archives.

"Where has this month gone? I can hardly believe we're almost into February," said Ruth when she arrived at Cathy's, for their Tuesday morning Mahjong session.

As Cathy served tea, coffee and muffins, Ruth shared news from the hospital.

"I spoke to Stella yesterday and she told me that Peter is recovering well. She sends her love to everyone. To be honest, I really think this accident could turn out to be a blessing in disguise as it seems to have brought the two of them much closer together."

Cathy responded, "Oh, that's wonderful news!"

Once again, she had a strong urge to share her own good news, but she managed to withhold it and focused instead on sharing details of her week's activities related to the case. The others followed suit and before long the brief WhatsApp messages that they'd been sharing all week long were supplemented with details until they were all fully updated.

"Right, let's get playing," said Sui Ling "or before we know it, we'll be out of time. I'm going to suggest we have a little topical game to begin with."

Ruth looked rather puzzled as she knew the game of Mahjong as well as Sui Ling but she couldn't guess what she meant by a 'topical game'.

Sui Ling soon clarified. "So, this morning I had an idea that instead of working on different hands, we start off by all working towards the same hand for the first game. I

143

was flicking through the Mahjong rule book and the hand called the 'Wriggly Snake' just popped out at me and I thought that this was an apt name for our murderer. It's interesting that it's also called the News Hand or the News Line-up and, of course, we're reading all the news reports that we can. On top of that, it's a concealed hand and very appropriate too as our culprit has been pretty good at concealing himself all of these years."

"Oh, I like the sound of that," said Ruth, "and, who knows, as we play ideas may be sparked that will eventually lead us to the snake's lair."

"So, what tiles do we need to collect to win the game, Sui Ling?" asked Cathy.

"Well, we all need a run of 1 to 9 in any one suit, plus one of each of the winds, North, East, West and South, to make up the word 'NEWS'. And we must pair a wind, any one of them will do."

"Okay, I've got it," Cathy replied as the others nodded signalling that they too understood.

Soon they were twittering the sparrows, building walls and playing to win this unusual round.

"Mahjong! I did it!" exclaimed Penny.

Ruth laughingly said, "I wonder if that means you're going to be the one to catch our elusive snake?"

Everyone laughed along as they shuffled the tiles creating the sound of twittering birds once again. They went on to play a few more games before lunch and a couple more afterwards, but by then it was time to call it a day.

Penny offered to host next week's game and, as she and Cathy walked towards their cars, they made arrangements to drive over to Arthur Fisher's place in the morning on the off chance they would find him in.

The next morning, as they neared his cottage, they could see smoke rising from the chimney and both were pleased that at last, they might actually get to talk to him.

"What if he doesn't want to talk to us," Cathy said.

"What if he does?" responded Penny. "Let's not look on the black side. He may be glad of a bit of company. Oh, I wish I'd brought some of the scones I made yesterday, but I didn't think. Well, it's too late now, we're here."

As Penny brought the car to a stop outside the cottage, Cathy could see an elderly man looking out of the window and, by the time they'd reached the door, they didn't even have to knock because Arthur Fisher had opened it wide and was saying hello before they could even introduce themselves.

"Can I help you?" he asked.

"I think so," said Penny who then went on to introduce both herself and Cathy.

"We're on a bit of a mission to find out more about the young girl who was murdered over in Bentham Woods twenty years ago and as you lived here back then, we thought you might be able to help us."

"Are you police officers?" Arthur asked.

"No, not at all. We're just part of a small group of friends who are trying to help bring closure for her family and everyone else. I know you were treated as a suspect at the time, but also know that you were released. Perhaps, like us, you'd like to see whoever was responsible brought to justice."

"I certainly would. Yes, I was a suspect for a short time, but my friends never thought for a minute that I was involved. Come in, please. I'm more than happy to talk to you and, to be honest, I'm ready to talk because it's a case that has never been far from my mind. Besides, I'm always glad of a little company."

Cathy joined in the conversation. "Thank you! It's good to know we share the same goal."

After he asked if they would like tea, Cathy offered to make it as she could see he was a little unsteady on his feet and Arthur seemed relieved to be able to sit down and let her busy herself in his kitchen. Anticipating having to wash the dishes, she was surprised, however, to see the kitchen looking like a new pin with everything in its place. Once they all had mugs of piping hot tea in hand, he explained that he'd only been home for a day.

"My sister, Annie, picked me up from the hospital yesterday morning and looked after me proper well until she left after dinner. She had to get back to York and her husband, Harry, you see because he's not too well himself these days. They've both been very good to me this past year. They used to visit once a week, at the weekends, but now Annie visits midweek too and each time, she gives this place a good going over. To be honest, I've just not had the energy to do much in the way of cleaning, so I'm really grateful for the help.

"Actually, I've got the big 'C' and the doctor tells me it's stage four so I'm not long for this world."

"I'm so sorry," responded Penny. "It's good that you have a sister who cares, but she does live a distance away, so I'm going to give you my number in case you need anything in a hurry because I'm only a short drive away in comparison."

"Please know that you can call me too," offered Cathy. "I don't live too far away either."

"That's so kind of you both. To be honest, Annie has given me this mobile thing. I told her, I've managed without a phone all my life and don't need one now, but she's a fuss pot and insisted that I have it even though I've no idea how to use it."

He laughed and Penny and Cathy joined in, the laughter breaking the tension that had been created as soon as Arthur had shared details of his condition.

Changing the subject, Cathy asked, "Can you tell us what you remember about the day that Gemma Davies' body was found?"

"I certainly can. I remember it as if it were yesterday and I'm going to get to why today because it's time for me to free myself up of the guilt I've been living with ever since."

Cathy and Penny looked at each other quizzically and wondered what might be coming next, but Arthur didn't seem to notice. He just continued talking.

"As usual, I was up bright and early that morning. I used to go out for a morning walk every day. I'm not able to do that anymore, of course, but back then I was as fit as a fiddle. I'd think nothing of walking five or even ten miles a day looking for good pieces of wood. I used to hunt for rabbits at the same time too. Oh, how I love a rabbit stew. Have you ever had rabbit stew?" he asked.

"No," they both replied.

"Ah, you don't know what you're missing. I think that's what I'll ask Annie to bring me the next time she comes over. She's a good girl. She prepares meals for me and puts them in the freezer so I don't have to do anything but defrost them and stick them in the microwave. She bought me the microwave too. She's into all these mod cons, but pretty clever things those microwaves, don't you think?"

Penny and Cathy realised that he was quite out of touch with the modern world given his comments on mobiles and microwaves, but they just decided to agree with him in the hopes of keeping him on track.

"I remember that morning in particular because all hell broke loose after the girl's body was found. A young couple said they'd spotted an older guy in the woods, but I never saw them. Anyway, the police questioned me."

"So, what happened next?" asked Cathy.

"Well, I could just tell you what I told the police, which is that I'd already collected enough wood and was on my way home where my day then carried on as normal. I used to carve animals and Annie and Harry would sell them for me. It's how I made a living back then as there was no shortage of buyers in York. For some reason, the tourists seemed to love my pieces. That's one of them," he said pointing to a wooden fox on the mantlepiece."

"Oh, that's wonderful. You're very talented," Penny responded, "but what do you mean when you said, I could just tell you what I told the police?"

"I mean that there's more to tell and I think now is the time to tell it."

Penny and Cathy exchanged quizzical glances, but, if Arthur saw this, he didn't let on. Instead, he asked Cathy to go into his bedroom, open the bottom drawer of the dresser and bring the box that she'd find at the back right hand side. Cathy did as he said and returned a couple of minutes later with a little nondescript brown cardboard box. Once it was in his hands, he continued to talk.

"On my way home, I found this half buried under leaves not too far from where the girl's body was found." He opened the box and brought out a piece of jewellery, but he clasped it in his hands, so at this point, neither of them could see it too well.

"I know I should have told the police about it, but I didn't."

"Why didn't you?" asked Cathy.

"Greed! Pure and simple greed. I told myself it didn't necessarily belong to the girl and I had it in mind that I could sell it, but not for myself, you understand. I kept it because I saw it as a way out for Annie and Harry. They're all right now, but, at the time, they were about to lose their home. They'd already lost their business and there seemed to be no way out for them and I thought my find could help them."

"But you never sold it. Why?" questioned Penny.

"Fear. I'm not a crook and what seemed like a good idea at the time, was not so good when it came to taking action. I never went near a jewellers with it; in fact, I stuffed it in that bottom drawer and it's been there ever since."

Penny interjected, "If you couldn't bring yourself to sell it, why didn't you just hand it in to the police?"

"It was just too late. I'd been questioned and had said nothing about it, and I figured that I might just become a real suspect if they discovered I'd got her necklace, if it was hers, of course."

He opened his hand and the piece of jewellery sparkled in the sunlight, but instead of admiring it, both Cathy and Penny were in shock. They both knew they were looking at Stella's long-lost necklace that they'd been talking about and admiring in her wedding photograph just a few short weeks ago, but, unlike Cathy, Penny feared she now knew the identity of the murderer.

Chapter 13

The Dilemma

After Penny explained that the necklace belonged to a friend of theirs, Arthur passed it over to her without hesitation saying, "Here, please take it. I've never had a minute's peace while it's been in my home and, if I could have a last wish, it would be that I could do something positive to help solve the murder of that young girl, especially if my actions prevented the case from being solved at the time. I know it might throw suspicion back on me, but I know I didn't do it and believe the truth will come out eventually."

Driving home with the necklace in hand, Cathy could barely hold her excitement.

"I can't wait to see Stella's face when we return the necklace to her."

"Cathy, let's just keep this to ourselves for now."

"What! Why?"

"I just want to dig a little deeper before we say anything to anyone. I can't explain right now, but, if you can just trust me for a couple of days, I think I might be able to get a few answers that will help in the long run."

"Okay, I'm itching to ask more, but I know you won't tell me. It's not a problem though, I trust you."

"Thank you, I promise to act quickly and hopefully will get the answers I need before the weekend."

In Leeds Infirmary, Peter was becoming stronger by the day and his relationship with Stella was also improving. The accident was really turning out to be a blessing in disguise.

"When I get out of here," said Peter, "I'm taking you back to Rome for a second honeymoon. Remember how we flew there the very night we were married and then strolled around hand in hand every day admiring the wonderful architecture."

"Oh, Peter, that sounds wonderful. Remember how we would stop at sidewalk cafes for coffees and slices of pizza? I remember we even threw three coins in the Trevi Fountain. I was so happy back then."

"You're going to be happy again. I know that I've not been the best of husbands, but that's going to change. At the point I thought I was going to die, I thought of you, and you, alone. It's not too late for us."

After Penny had dropped Cathy off in the village, she headed straight home and started to think about how best to deal with her suspicions given her own history with Peter. The last thing she wanted was to have that raked up or cause suffering to Stella, especially if she was putting two and two together and coming up with five. She decided that visiting Peter alone would be the best thing to do. She didn't waste time and called Stella immediately.

"Hi Stella, it's me, Penny. How are you and how's Peter doing?"

"Oh, it's lovely to hear your voice. I'm missing you all so much, but, thankfully, Peter's doing really well. To tell you the truth, we both are, as this accident seems to have changed him back into the man I used to know."

"We're all missing you too and can't wait for you to join us again. I'm glad to hear Peter is recovering well. Are you still staying with him in the hospital?"

"Not overnight anymore, but I spend every day with him. I head home before dark because the sleeping arrangements here are pretty much non-existent. Three nights on his bedside chair were more than enough!"

"I can imagine. It must be lonely for you at home, so if you ever want any company in the evenings or even at the hospital, let me know, I'll be more than happy to join you."

"Thank you, but I'm really okay. I'm just loving having Peter all to myself. We're sharing our memories of good times past and Peter's even suggested we go on a second honeymoon when he's well enough. I've not been as happy as I am now for a long time. Marcus is coming over this weekend, so I was thinking of giving him some alone time with Peter and inviting the girls over for morning coffee on Saturday. Would you be free to come?"

"That sounds lovely. I'll definitely be there. Let me know if I can do anything to help."

"Thank you, but I'll get Brenda to help me. She loves it when we entertain and impromptu get-togethers don't faze her at all. Seriously, I can't imagine anyone has a better housekeeper than me when it comes to catering."

Penny laughed. "Well, she's better than mine given that I don't have one! Okay, I'll see you on Saturday about ten, yes?"

"Perfect," Stella replied. "See you then."

At five o'clock the following day, Penny was on the road to Leeds. It was good timing not only because she knew Stella wouldn't be at the hospital, but also because Gregory was on duty until ten o'clock so he wouldn't even miss her.

No one was more surprised than Peter when Penny walked into his hospital room. The frosty relationship that they'd managed to hide so well in public was hardly one that he imagined would bring Penny visiting.

"To what do I owe this pleasure?" Peter said.

"I have to talk to you about something important," Penny replied.

"Really, what's that?"

Penny then began to relay all that had happened when she and Cathy had met Arthur. Peter paled, when she spoke of the necklace.

"Now, I'm obviously wondering why Stella's necklace would turn up in the woods near the body of that murdered girl. I could have gone straight to the police but decided for Stella's sake to give you the benefit of the doubt and hear what you have to say first because I know it's possible for there to be no connection. I need to hear your explanation for myself."

"There's no connection whatsoever and, if you're suggesting that I'm a murderer, you must be out of your mind."

"I don't know what to think because I know for myself that you're not averse to having extra-marital affairs."

"That may be so, but that doesn't mean that I'm a murderer!"

"Well, it seems more than a coincidence that the missing necklace was found not only in those woods, but so near to the girl's body. Surely, you've got to admit that! And let's be honest, I of all people know only too well that giving jewellery gifts to your flings fits the pattern of your behaviour, although I must say that giving a family heirloom seems to be going just a bit too far. Actually, it's the only reason I'm here now and not with the police."

"Look, we've both got things to hide, but I can assure you that I'm no murderer, so why don't we just forget about the necklace. In fact, you could make it disappear if you want to and no-one would be any the wiser."

Penny was quick to respond, "What! If you think I'm ever going to be a part of your deception again, you've got another think coming. The main person I want to protect here is Stella, but I'm not going to lie even to do that. It seems I have little choice now, but to go to the police and, let's face it, if you didn't kill her you have nothing to fear."

"I have a great deal to fear and so do you because we both have marriages that could end if you take this any further."

"What do you mean?"

"I think you know very well what I mean because if you go to the police with this and Stella learns of my infidelity, I'm not going to keep it a secret that you were one of those 'flings' as you call it."

"Are you threatening me?"

"Stella may have had suspicions about my lack of fidelity, but I've never rubbed her face in it. We're getting on just fine now, better than ever to be honest and I don't want her hurt through having her suspicions confirmed just when she's so happy and looking forward to our future together. So, if you're asking me if this is a threat, the answer is yes! I'm not going to let you destroy my life while you carry on with your little charade at home with Gregory."

"You low life! You took advantage of me when I was vulnerable. How dare you now threaten to destroy my marriage."

Without giving Peter a chance to reply, she turned to go, but, as she reached the door, she looked back at him and snapped. "Gregory is twice the man you will ever be!"

If Peter was in turmoil at this point, so was Penny. Driving home gave her time to think. She was so angry at Peter and his threat. Even though his reaction had convinced her that he was not the murderer, her years of dislike for him remained and she fought against her desire to simply retaliate. Rather, she knew that whatever she did, she had to do it for the right reasons.

She played over their conversation and knew there was no way she could simply forget about the necklace as Peter had suggested. Not only could doing so implicate her in a murder if he did turn out to be guilty, but it would destroy the only bit of new evidence that had come to light to help them to solve the case. Besides, she knew Cathy was fully aware of the necklace and waiting for answers, so hiding the only real clue they had was not an option. She gripped the steering wheel tightly as her anger at Peter's threat boiled up inside. However, by the time she arrived home, she knew she could not let the threat stop her from doing what was right, even if it would put her marriage at risk. No, she knew there was only one thing to do.

By the time Gregory arrived home, she was already in bed and knew this was not the right time to talk to him. After late shifts at the hospital, he was always shattered, so as he climbed into bed beside her, she feigned sleep as she couldn't trust herself not to let everything tumble out.

However, she was up bright and early the next morning

and had made a special effort to prepare Gregory's favourite breakfast even before he put in an appearance.

"What have I done to deserve this?" Gregory asked as he walked into the kitchen.

"Can't a wife treat her husband without having an ulterior motive?" she replied.

Laughingly, he said, "I know you too well; come on, out with it."

"All right, I do want to talk to you, but not until you can give me your undivided attention. Maybe tonight, if you don't have a late shift."

"Yes, tonight's good. I'll be home by six thirty, and I'm yours for the rest of the evening. I must say, I'm intrigued though. Can't you give me a clue? You're not pregnant, are you?"

"Of course not, do you think I'd want another baby after my experience of being pregnant with the twins! There's no way I'd want to go through that again."

"That's a relief! So, you're not going to give me a clue?"

"No, you'll just have to be patient until tonight. I'll cook a special dinner. Have you got any requests?"

"No, I'll leave it to you. I'd better get a move on as I've a full day ahead of me with every appointment slot filled and hardly time to eat lunch, although after this breakfast and the promise of a special dinner, maybe I can skip lunch altogether."

Once Gregory had left, Penny busied herself with housework and shopping before heading off to her exercise class, but all the time her mind was in turmoil as she played over how best to tell Gregory news that he wouldn't want to hear.

By six o'clock, dinner was ready and the house looked as neat as a pin but, with half an hour still to go, Penny was on edge. She went through to the kitchen and somewhat out of character, she poured herself a large brandy. She thought she was sipping it slowly, but in less than ten minutes her glass was empty. She headed back to the kitchen for a refill, but hesitated when she picked up the bottle, knowing that alcohol was not the answer and the last thing she needed was muddle-headed thinking when she explained everything to Gregory. Thankfully, at that very moment, she heard his car pull into the drive and she quickly popped a mint into her mouth in the hopes of disguising the smell of alcohol on her breath.

"Hi!" Gregory said as he walked into the room. "How's your day been?"

"Fine," Penny replied. "You're early. I didn't think you'd be home for another twenty minutes. Was your day not as busy as you'd expected?"

"Busier actually! I had to deal with two emergency cases on top of everything else today, but my last appointment was cancelled. Now, I'm ready for that special dinner you promised me because I didn't get a bite to eat all day and I'm famished! What are we having?"

"Rib-eye steak with mushrooms and crispy potatoes and for dessert your favourite lemon meringue pie."

"Wonderful! Give me two minutes to get changed and I'll be ready to feast."

The dinner was cooked to perfection and Gregory enjoyed every mouthful, but, to Penny, everything tasted like cardboard. Her mouth was dry and eating was the last thing she needed. She felt tense and wondered if Gregory could sense this. If he did, he certainly didn't show it. He did most of the talking, but, other than nodding in all the right places, Penny barely said a word, for she was more preoccupied with the conversation to come. As Gregory leaned back in his chair after his last bite, he said, "Come on then, out with it. What do you want to talk to me about?"

"Can you make a pot of coffee while I clear away and then we can talk," responded Penny.

"This sounds very serious," Gregory responded as he dutifully set about making the coffee, but Penny didn't answer.

When they sat down together with drinks in hand, she began to talk.

"You remember how you asked me if I was pregnant this morning and I said, I'd never want to go through that again? Do you know what I was driving at?"

"Of course, I know how terribly you suffered with postnatal depression and I wouldn't want you to go through that again either."

Penny continued, "You remember how it nearly destroyed our marriage and that we were distant for a long time after I came out of the hospital?"

"Yes," Gregory replied questioningly.

"Well, throughout that whole time, I wasn't myself. Even though they'd let me come home, I felt scared and alone and you seemed so cold towards me."

She could see Gregory stiffen and she quickly said, "I'm not trying to make excuses, but just explain my feelings because they led me to act in a way that I will regret for the rest of my life."

"Penny, you're making me tense. Please get to the point!"

"It's not easy because I know that what I'm going to say will hurt you and may hurt our marriage too, and I really don't want that to happen."

Gregory just nodded.

"I need to go back to when I was suffering from postnatal depression after having the twins. You remember when I came out of hospital and the boys were still being looked after by your mum, you went away for three days to attend a medical conference."

Again, Gregory nodded.

"Well, I answered the door just a few hours after you left

and found Peter and Stella standing there with flowers. They said they'd just popped by to wish me well and to ask if they could help in any way. It was very timely because on top of feeling sad and alone, I was also struggling to unblock the kitchen sink. I told them and Peter went straight in to see if he could help. He couldn't, but he offered to come back later with a plunger.

"He came back about an hour later, and it didn't take him very long to sort out because the plunger did the trick. He didn't rush off though because I'd made him a coffee while he was working and he sat down to drink it afterwards. He then asked for a second cup and, before I knew it, more than two hours had passed. He was such a good listener and I just poured my heart out to him. He left after giving me a hug and telling me everything would be all right. I felt so comforted.

"I guess that should have been the end of it, but the next morning, I found him on our doorstep again. He told me he was just checking up on me and that he'd do so each day until you returned. That second day, we sat on the sofa and as I poured my heart out again, he put his arm around my shoulder and that touched me in such a way that I ended up just breaking down and crying non-stop. He hugged me as I cried and before I knew it, he was kissing me. I know he shouldn't have and that I should have stopped him, but I felt so safe in his arms that I just couldn't bring myself to pull away. One thing led to another and I don't need to tell you what happened next, do I?

"Afterwards, I was shocked by my own actions, but, at that time, I felt I just couldn't stop myself. I hate telling you this, but it didn't end there; it turned into an affair, I guess you'd call it, which lasted right up until the day you came home with flowers for me on our wedding anniversary. That day, you were so loving and it hit me there and then what a fool I'd been. I called Peter the next morning and told him that it was over and that we'd betrayed you and Stella in the worst way imaginable. He didn't argue; in fact, I discovered later that I was not his first extramarital affair. After calling him, I parcelled up a bracelet that he'd given to me and posted it to his office with no return address. From that day to this, I've had little respect for him because I believe he took advantage of me at a low point in my life, but, as I talk about it now, I realise he probably fell into the situation too. I don't believe he came looking for an affair any more than I did."

She'd held her head down throughout, but glanced up as she'd finished and, although she saw Gregory looking straight at her, he didn't say a word. Maybe only a minute passed, but it felt like a lifetime to Penny.

"Gregory, please say something," she whispered.

Chapter 14

The Heartbreak

To Penny, Gregory's silence seemed to last an age and that in itself was painful, but, when he spoke, she felt even worse.

"I don't trust myself to speak," Gregory replied. "I need time on my own right now. I'm going to pack a small bag and I'll call you tomorrow."

"Gregory, you can't leave at this time of night. Please let's talk."

"No, not yet. I really need time to think. I'll just check into the Premier Inn near the hospital and ring you tomorrow."

As Gregory drove away, Penny was heartbroken. She hated having hurt him in this way, but she knew she had no choice and it was definitely better coming from her than anyone else. She went to bed, but it was a long night as her mind kept going over the evening and what must now be done. She eventually drifted off to sleep through sheer emotional exhaustion just as dawn was beginning to break.

She woke at ten in the morning to the distant sound of her mobile ringing. She quickly went downstairs to find it, but, by the time she did, it was too late. She could see the missed call was from Gregory so she rang him back immediately, but there was no answer. Just then, a message popped up from him saying, 'Just to let you know I'm at work and will be home this evening.'

Penny responded by quickly typing, 'Okay, will have something ready for dinner. Love you.'

Relief that he was coming home quickly turned into worry about what he might say. She didn't want this marriage to end and hoped he wouldn't too, but she knew this was a possibility and out of her control.

Her mind turned back to the necklace and her need to talk to Ruth because she figured she would be the best one to know what to do about this new-found evidence. Still, she also knew that she must put her relationship with Gregory first; therefore, she decided not to call Ruth or anyone else until after she and Gregory had talked and, instead, she busied herself around the house to pass the time.

Sui Ling was busying herself at home too. She was updating her file by adding all the information they'd gathered among them from contacts with Gemma's parents and friend as well as her ex-boyfriend and Charlie Statham. She pored over the completed file hoping for a light bulb moment, but so far was drawing a blank.

Meanwhile, on the road to Leeds to visit Peter, Ruth and Stella were deep in conversation.

"He's become like a different man, Ruth. Honestly, it seems crazy to say, but this accident has been one of the best things that has ever happened to our marriage. It's even brought Peter and Marcus closer."

"I'm so happy for you," responded Ruth, "and I'm looking forward to seeing Peter again. Oh, and I'm really looking forward to Saturday morning too. What would you like me to bring?" she asked.

"Nothing, really, I want to treat you girls. It's my way of saying thank you for being such great supporters. I really couldn't have managed without you, especially through those first few days and, as for the investigation, I'm just grateful that you've all stepped up without making me feel guilty that I've not been pulling my weight."

"Oh, my goodness, it's only right for you to have been by Peter's side throughout. You don't owe us thanks for that, but I'm still looking forward to Saturday," Ruth said with a smile.

After Stella's positive report, Ruth expected to find an upbeat Peter when she walked into his hospital room, but, instead, she experienced a flat greeting in response to her cheery hello. Stella was equally concerned, for Peter seemed distant and preoccupied, certainly not the man she'd left in the hospital room just yesterday afternoon.

Stella spoke. "Peter, what's wrong? You've been so happy of late, but now you look drawn and unhappy. What's happened? Please tell me because I'm beginning to worry now."

Peter was not about to share that Penny had been to visit him or that what she'd told him was causing him inner turmoil. "Don't worry. I'm just a little tired. It may be the drugs I'm taking."

"Has the doctor given you some new meds because you've been fine on the ones you've been taking? In fact, he was saying that you'd soon be off pain killers altogether. I'm confused. Do you want me to speak to him for you?"

"No, I'll talk to him. I just feel a little down; it may be that everything is just beginning to dawn on me," he lied.

Ruth joined in the conversation. "Yes, sometimes the shock of an event can take a while to surface. At least you're in the right place to get help."

"Yes, yes, of course, that must be it," said Stella eager to find a solution because the last thing she wanted to do was lose the man she felt she'd only just started to find again.

"I think you're right, Ruth," Peter replied. "Actually, I'm really tired this morning and just not good company. Would you ladies mind if I asked you to leave for a couple of hours at least so I can get some sleep? I'm not sleeping well right now and I feel totally drained."

Without hesitation, Stella answered, "All right, we'll come back this afternoon. Maybe we can go shopping, I want to get some bits for your birthday celebration anyway."

"Oh, please, Stella, I really don't want a celebration, not this year. If I'm out of here by then, I just want a quiet time at home."

"I think that sounds very sensible," joined in Ruth. "We can go shopping for treats for us instead, Stella. That will be fun, and maybe we can have a spot of lunch in town too. Would that be all right with you, Peter, because I'm sure it will take us more than a couple of hours?"

"Yes, of course," he replied. "To be honest, the more time I have to sleep the better."

After saying farewell, Stella and Ruth headed out of the door leaving Peter alone with his thoughts.

Cathy was alone with her thoughts too. She was puzzling over why Penny wanted to delay sharing news of the necklace with the girls. She was so eager to tell all and share what seemed to be an amazing breakthrough. Nevertheless, she had given her word and wouldn't break it.

Her mind then turned to all things baby related and the rush of excitement she felt was overwhelming. She was so looking forward to sharing news of her pregnancy with the girls on Saturday at Stella's coffee morning. In fact, that made her think of making a coffee for herself and, five minutes later, she was sitting in front of the computer, hot cup of coffee in hand, searching for baby names to add to the list that she and Dan had already started.

Less than two miles away, Penny was not so at peace. She had been pacing the floor on tenterhooks for at least half an hour by the time Gregory arrived home. She didn't know whether to run and hug him or to wait for him to say something, but, unable to stand silence of any kind right now, she welcomed him warmly.

"I missed you last night and have thought of nothing else but us and our marriage all day. I do so want everything to be all right."

"Well, I've had plenty of time to think and I do want to talk. In fact, I'd like us to do that before we even think about eating. Is that all right with you?"

"Yes, yes, of course. I've made a stew so it will be fine whatever time we want to eat."

Together they went into the lounge which was warm and cheery on a cold winter's night, but neither of them felt comforted by this. They sat at either end of the sofa both wrapped up in their own fears.

With his stomach churning, Gregory began to speak and, in a soft voice, said "I guess we've both been keeping secrets from each other."

Penny, quickly answered, "I'm so sorry, Gregory. I've regretted my actions ever since and you have no idea how many times I've wished I could turn the clock back and change the past."

"I know but let me finish. I've been thinking about how much you suffered and have come to regret putting my work before you at that time. Not just because of you turning to someone else, but because I failed you when you needed me the most. I also wish I could turn the clock back and have been the man you needed me to be. I thought I was doing the right thing at the time by working extra hours to provide for you and the twins, but I did realise I'd got my priorities all wrong when our wedding anniversary came around that year. That's why I booked the spa weekend away for us. It breaks my heart that I didn't wake up sooner. If I had, neither of us would have to live with what happened."

"I so loved that day you came home with the flowers and the gift of a spa weekend, Gregory. It actually touched me so much that it brought me back to my senses, and I can assure you that after breaking the relationship off with Peter I've kept my distance from him ever since."

"I always thought you were rather cool with him but had no idea why. I'm not going to blame you, as I believe I'm just as much to blame in my own way, but I don't know right now what I'm going to do about Peter. Still, I do know that I love you and I want us to work through this."

"Oh, Gregory, I love you and want that too. Thank you for being you."

Penny moved across the sofa and put her arms around Gregory and they clung tightly to each other. As tears fell from Penny's eyes, Gregory gently kissed her and whispered words that she could only have dreamt of hearing when all alone with her thoughts last night. The darkness had been not only physical but mental too as she'd feared her marriage might be ending.

Now, feeling secure in Gregory's arms, Penny suddenly realised that he'd been working all day and probably hadn't even had time for lunch. "Oh, my goodness," she said. "You must be starving. Let me go and heat up the stew and we can eat. I actually want to talk to you about what Cathy and I discovered when we met with Arthur

Fisher yesterday."

"I could certainly do with that stew. Did you make dumplings to go with it too?"

"Would I ever make stew for you without dumplings when I know you love them so much?" Smiling, she continued, "You know the old saying, the way to a man's heart is through his stomach!"

After dinner, Penny shared every detail of the visit she and Cathy had made to Arthur Fisher and then more reluctantly she spoke of her subsequent visit to see Peter and her need to share all with the girls.

"I'm not too happy about your sharing details of your past relationship with Peter," he said.

"I'm hoping I don't have to. To be honest, I wanted it dead and buried and wouldn't even have shared it with you because I never wanted to cause you pain. It was only Peter's threat and knowing I couldn't hide the truth about the necklace that I realised I had no choice but to tell you. To my mind, I've always figured it was my burden to carry. Now, I might be the one breaking Stella's heart, too, because even if Peter is telling the truth, and he had nothing to do with the girl's murder, his affair with her is bound to come out. When it does, there's no knowing whether Peter will take this out on me causing my involvement with him to become public knowledge too."

"I agree, you've no choice, but we'll face whatever we have to face together," Gregory assured her.

Penny couldn't believe how wonderful he was being. It was more than she'd dared hope for or deserved, and she was prompted by his words to repeat the words she'd shared with Peter. "Gregory, you are twice the man that Peter will ever be and I'm so proud to be your wife."

Early the next morning, Penny drove to Ruth's to tell her about the find ahead of the get-together at Stella's. She wanted to ask Ruth's advice on what to do now that they had Stella's necklace. However, Penny couldn't bring herself to share about her meeting with Peter, but that seemed immaterial at this stage. Her main concern was for Stella and the devastating effect it would have if Peter were to become a suspect again, which was more than likely to happen.

"I don't think we have any choice but to tell her, Penny," said Ruth. "I'm sure he will be questioned again, but let's hope that there's a simple explanation that shows him to be innocent. Do you have the necklace with you?"

"Yes. Should we give it back to her or do you think it should be handed over to the police?"

"I would like to say we should give it back to her, but I think we need to get the police involved because the necklace could well be key to unlocking this mystery. I'll ask George what we should do."

As Ruth was calling George, Penny called Cathy to let her know about the conversation she'd just had with Ruth.

"George is going to join us at eleven o'clock," reported Ruth, "and he said not to handle the necklace any more than is necessary because apparently, even after all this time, it can hold evidence that might help. He asked me to lock it in the safe in his study."

Penny realized, at this point, that she was just too close to the whole situation and she didn't trust herself to be able to share news of the find in the best way, so she asked Ruth if she would be the one to take the lead in sharing the news at Stella's. Ruth agreed and they headed off, but despite being early, they actually found themselves the last to arrive.

"Well, we thought we might be the first to get here," said Ruth. Laughingly she continued, "I guess we're all just eager to be in each other's company again!"

Despite the fact that Cathy couldn't wait to see Stella's face when told that she and Penny had located the missing necklace, her mind was really on her own news. So, as soon as the greetings were over and everyone had moved into the kitchen for hot drinks, she made her announcement.

"Girls, I've got some exciting news that I've been bursting to tell you since Christmas, but Dan kept reminding me we needed to keep it to ourselves until this week."

By the time Cathy had finished saying these words, they all knew what to expect next, but no one was about to steal the moment from her.

"I'm pregnant!" she said with so much excitement in her voice that it was infectious. Immediately, congratulations rang around the room.

"Wonderful!" said Ruth. "That makes two babies for me to knit for now."

Penny joined in, "Oh, I'm so happy for you. When is your sweet bundle due?"

"Mid-July," Cathy replied.

"Oh, I must introduce you to my daughter-in-law as you're only about six weeks behind her. The next time they join us for Sunday lunch, you and Dan must come over too," invited Ruth.

"That sounds wonderful. I'd love to meet her. I don't know anyone else who is pregnant."

Sui Ling, being her ever practical self, said, "Don't worry, when you connect into the system, you'll find yourself surrounded by expectant mums. I was a relatively new wife in a new country when I became pregnant, but I soon found myself with a supportive network after starting prenatal classes at the hospital."

Cathy shared that it seemed to be happening already. "Last night I joined a Facebook group of mums-to-be and by the time I got up this morning, I'd already received a couple of congratulatory messages from other expectant mums. It's exciting, but not the same as talking with someone face-to-face, so I'd still love to meet your daughter-in-law, Ruth."

"Isn't technology amazing?" said Stella. "Of course, we didn't have anything like that when I was pregnant with Marcus, but I agree with Sui Ling, you'll find lots of support once you start getting involved with what's on offer. Besides, you've got us too, and I for one am going to love being one of your baby's local 'grandmas'."

After the excitement of the baby talk had died down, Ruth spoke, "Well, ladies, I think we should talk about the case now because there has been a pretty major development. Cathy and Penny managed to catch Arthur Fisher at home this week and you'll never believe this, Stella. Your missing necklace has been in his possession ever since the day of the murder!"

"What! How can that be?"

"Well, he has his own story to tell which I'm sure the police will check out because it's certainly time for us to involve them. I spoke with George about it this morning; in fact, I hope you don't mind, but I invited him to come round at eleven, Stella, so that he can advise us where to go from here."

At that very moment, there was a knock on the door.

Chapter 15

The Arrests

Stella answered the door, "Oh, George, Ruth has just been telling me that my necklace has been found and that it's been with Arthur Fisher all these years. Do you think this means that he killed the girl?"

"It's possible, of course, but, until we investigate more thoroughly, I have to keep an open mind," George responded. "All I can say at this stage is that Arthur will be brought in for questioning along with everyone who has some connection with the necklace."

"Well, who else is connected?" Stella asked. "As far as I can see, there's only Peter and I, but it belonged to us, so we wouldn't have been the ones to steal it."

"So, you believe it was stolen?" he queried.

"Well what other explanation can there be? Oh, look at me, I'm being so rude questioning you before you've even had a chance to take your coat off and say hello to everyone. Please come through and sit down and let me offer you a hot drink."

George followed her into the living room and warmly greeted everyone before sitting down.

"Now what would you like to drink, my best Yorkshire tea, fresh coffee or even hot chocolate?" Stella asked.

177

"A cup of your best Yorkshire tea would be perfect," said George with a smile.

After Stella returned with George's tea and took a seat herself, he brought the conversation back to the necklace.

"I must admit ladies that I was sceptical when Ruth told me of your intentions to become amateur sleuths, but I have to hand it to you, you've done a sterling job in uncovering just what we needed to get the official investigation motoring again. Of course, this means that we will be handling the case from this point on, but I don't want to shut any of you out, so if you ladies have any ideas that you want to share with me, I promise, I'll be ready to listen at any time."

"When do you think I could have my necklace back, George?" asked Stella.

"Once the case is wrapped up for sure, but, right now, I can't tell you when that will be. I can tell you what we plan to do though. First of all, two officers are already on their way to interview Mr. Fisher and, depending upon what he tells us, we may have others to interview too. Certainly, Stella, we'll need to talk to you and Peter. How is he doing now? Do you think he would be up to answering a few questions?"

"Well, yesterday he was not as bright and cheerful as he has been. He mentioned that he's not been sleeping well, but to be honest, I think he'll be so pleased to hear that the necklace has been found, he'll be eager to talk and discover how it came to be in Arthur Fisher's hands."

When the two officers sent to interview Arthur arrived at his home, they found him compliant and willing to talk. However, he could tell them no more than he'd told Penny and Cathy. If Arthur thought it would end there, he was sadly mistaken though because when asked if he could provide an alibi for the day on which Gemma had been murdered, he couldn't. While there was insufficient evidence to arrest him for murder at this stage, he was told that he was being arrested for withholding evidence and that he would have to accompany them to the police station.

When Ruth called George to ask him to pick up some milk on his way home that day, he said that he would actually like to have an informal chat with Stella and asked Ruth if she could accompany him in the afternoon.

"Of course, I can. I will head over at whatever time you want."

"Good, I'll call you when I'm on my way."

"Are you going to tell her you're coming?"

"Yes, I'm going to give her a call now, but I just wanted to check that you'd be free to go with me, first."

"Okay, I'll see you soon."

Ruth was the first to arrive, but, true to his promise, George had already called ahead and Stella was expecting her.

"Do you know what he wants to talk to me about, Ruth?"

"Not really, but I expect he has questions that he didn't want to ask when everyone was here this morning. He just asked me to come along to keep you company."

"Oh, here he is now!" Stella said, as she saw George's car pulling up outside.

For the second time in a matter of hours, Stella welcomed George into her home and offered him a drink. Once all three of them had a cup of tea in hand, he got straight to the point.

"Stella, I'm trying to get to the bottom of how the necklace ended up with Arthur Fisher and, of course, the first place to start is to find out how and when it left your home. Can you tell me when you first realised it was gone and what you did about it, because I can't find a report of it being stolen?"

"Oh, it was many years ago, obviously. I wanted to wear it one evening and just couldn't find it. I must admit I'm a little careless with jewellery when I get home from evenings out. I rarely put my things straight away and have been known to leave earrings and other items on the coffee table, in the kitchen or bathroom or sometimes by my bedside. I was puzzled though because Brenda is a gem and she tidies up after me, so I can usually find things in their right place when I want them."

"So, when it didn't turn up, why didn't you report it as stolen?", George asked.

"I wanted to, but Peter knows how scatty I am and said that it would probably turn up and that it would just be a waste of police time; besides, there had been no evidence of a break in. Sadly, though, it never did turn up and I guess we just felt we'd left it far too long to make a report. Actually, I still harboured hopes of it surfacing one day but never in this way."

"So, how do you think it could have ended up in Bentham Woods?" he asked.

"I really have no idea. I suppose someone could have stolen it while visiting the house because I certainly trust Brenda."

"Is there anyone else who has access to the house?"

"Well, there's Diana, but she didn't work for us at the time. She started around fifteen years ago when we felt Brenda needed a little help with the housework."

"Diana?" George queried.

"Yes, Diana Staunton. She lives in the village."

"Ah, yes, I know who you mean. She has a boy, what's his name?"

"It's Johnny and he works here, too, helping Eric with the gardens, but he doesn't have access to the house. Besides, he's only been working here for two years."

"So, the only person who had keys back then was Brenda, right?"

"Yes, that's right."

"I might need to ask you more questions, but I'd like to speak to Brenda and Peter. Would it be possible to speak to Brenda now?"

"I'm sure she'll be willing to talk to you, but this is her weekend off. Bless her, she was up very early this morning to help me in the kitchen when she needn't have done. She and Eric actually left as soon as she'd helped me clear away after our coffee morning. They've gone to visit Brenda's sister and won't be back until late tomorrow, so maybe you could come back on Monday to talk to her if that's okay with you."

"Yes, of course, now when do you think would be the best time for me to speak to Peter? I'd like to speak to him alone if you don't mind."

"How about tomorrow as he's had Marcus with him all day, so he'll probably be tired at this stage? Marcus and I can spend the morning together and only visit in the afternoon. I know it's a Sunday, but would that work for you?"

"Yes, no problem at all, I'm used to working all hours as Ruth can tell you."

"Oh, when you say 'working' that makes it sound very official George."

"Don't worry, Stella. It's just routine. I'll make sure I leave him before twelve so that you and Marcus can visit in the afternoon."

"Thank you, now can I get you a top up of tea?"

"No, I must be on my way as I've got commitments, but Ruth may be free to stay a while."

"I'd love another cuppa," Ruth responded.

"Okay, I'll leave you ladies now, but thanks for your time, Stella."

"Thank you for trying to get to the bottom of this for us. I really appreciate it, George."

By ten o'clock the next morning, George was entering Peter's hospital room.

"Hi, George, Stella told me the good news about the necklace and that you'd be popping in to see me today."

"Yes, it's quite a find and, hopefully, it will help us to get to the bottom of this case, but first, how are you doing? Are you likely to be going home any time soon?"

"I'm definitely on the mend and with a bit of luck, I'll be heading home later this week. I'll be in a wheelchair for a while, but the doctor thinks I'll be walking again before too long."

"That's good news. I bet you can't wait to get home and into your own bed, not to mention having some good home-cooked food too. Now, as Stella will have told you, I'm trying to piece things together and work out how the necklace got from your home to Bentham Woods."

After Peter relayed pretty much the same story as Stella had told him yesterday, George went on to ask a few questions that he hadn't put to Stella.

"I understand what you're saying, but here's my biggest concern. We know from her friend, Sharon, that Gemma was seeing someone quite wealthy. As you know, the officers handling the case at that time, questioned you and the rest of the men in the area who owned Range Rovers because of the tyre markings that were discovered not too far from where her body was found."

"Yes, I remember," Peter responded.

"The thing that troubles me now and gives a connection that was missing at the time is the necklace. Obviously, it didn't walk there by itself and it's reasonable to surmise that it was being worn by Gemma Davies at the time of her murder."

"I see the connection you're trying to make, but, seriously, a girl wearing a necklace like that for a regular night out seems very unlikely and, although she may have been wearing it, you need to consider finding it there is nothing more than a coincidence."

"Yes, of course that's possible, but it's my job to find out which of the two scenarios is the most plausible. I'm puzzling at this stage about how a necklace that belongs to Stella could possibly have come to be in the girl's possession. I know for sure from the reports that she was attacked beside the car and then dragged to where her body was found and that the necklace was actually discovered close by. To me this suggests that it's more likely to have been worn by her as opposed to being unconnected.

"So, my concern, Peter, is that the links to you seem strong. Let me put it this way, the necklace belongs to your family, you are a rich man and you owned a Range Rover at the time. Can you see where I'm coming from?"

"Yes, I suppose it doesn't look too good for me when you put it that way, but I had nothing to do with her murder. I may be many things, but I'm certainly not a killer."

"You're spot on. It's not looking good for you right now, but there's a way that I can arrange for you to be eliminated as a potential suspect."

"What do you mean? How?"

"Well, you could volunteer to have a DNA test as we do have some, as yet unidentified DNA taken from her body that we've always hoped would one day lead us to her murderer."

"I'm sorry, George, but I'm not going to volunteer to take a test as I don't think it would be in my best interests. I really don't want to say anything more, but I can assure you that I'm not guilty."

George was more than a little surprised when Peter refused to take the DNA test when it could so obviously clear his name. This raised in George, the nagging doubts that he'd suppressed, given that Peter and Stella were close friends. Could Peter be the murderer after all? George felt there was little else that could be said at this point, so he thanked Peter for answering his questions and said he'd be back if there was a need. Both men then said their farewells with inner tensions that both did their best to conceal.

Ruth could see that George was troubled when he returned from visiting Peter, but, when she tried to probe, he was very guarded and gave nothing away.

On Monday morning, George left for work earlier than usual and Ruth had a foreboding that left her feeling quite uneasy. She gave Stella a call, but she didn't seem at all concerned.

"Hi Stella, how are you doing?" Ruth asked.

"Oh, I'm doing just great. Marcus has agreed to stay for a few days instead of flying out this afternoon. I can't tell you how happy that makes me feel."

"Oh, I can imagine. I'm guessing you won't want to play Mahjong tomorrow?"

"Do you mind? I want to savour every moment with my boy."

"Of course not. I think everyone else will be coming over, so we'll have a table of four. We did agree it would be at my place, didn't we? I honestly don't know where I am these days," she added.

Stella laughed. "Yes, we did. It's not like you to forget anything. Are you okay?"

"Yes, yes, I'm fine. I've just got a lot on my mind at the moment. You have a nice time with Marcus and I'll see you soon."

"Thank you, but remember, I'm here for you too if you need to talk and Marcus would certainly understand, so don't hesitate to let me know if I can help."

"Thank you, Stella. I'll see you soon."

After quick calls to all the ladies to ask how they were doing and if they would be coming to play Mahjong tomorrow, Ruth got on with preparations: a little cleaning and baking.

In George's office, a meeting was already underway. He'd called together a small team of senior officers to talk about the case and the possible next steps. His Deputy Chief Constable, John Clayton, was the first to suggest a viable course of action.

"From what you've said, George, we haven't enough evidence to mount a case against him in court, but I think we've got sufficient circumstantial evidence and some reasonable grounds for making an arrest and bringing him in for questioning. As you know, we then have the power to compel him to take a DNA test, which we should certainly do because his refusal to take a voluntary test suggests to me that we may have our man."

The team agreed and George approved the plan. However, John suggested that George should now step back and let him be the one to arrest Peter. This made sense to George because he would advise others to step back from cases where a personal relationship exists in order to protect all involved. George chose two officers to go with John to the hospital. He knew it would not be possible for them to take Peter into custody after the arrest due to his incapacity, so stationing officers outside Peter's hospital room would be absolutely necessary.

John entered Peter's room that afternoon accompanied by the two officers and, after introducing himself and briefly giving the reason for his visit, he arrested Peter by reading him his rights.

"Peter Benchley-Smythe, you are under arrest on suspicion of the murder of Gemma Davies. You do not have to say anything, but it may harm your defence if you do not mention when questioned something which you later rely on in court. Anything you do say may be given in evidence."

Chapter 16

The Confession

Peter was visibly shaken, but focused himself, by concentrating upon his rights.

"I'd like to make the call that I'm entitled to before we go any further."

"Of course. Please go ahead," replied John.

"Stella, you're not going to believe this, but I'm under arrest!"

"What! What on earth for?"

"They've made the preposterous accusation that I murdered the girl found in Bentham Woods!"

"I thought they'd arrested Arthur Fisher."

"I don't know, but this is very real and I need you to get in touch with Michael and let him know what's happened. Please ask him to get over here as soon as possible."

"Oh, I wish Marcus and I hadn't left you early today. Can we come back now?"

"No, I'm afraid I won't be allowed to see anyone, but my legal representative which is why I want you to get hold of Michael without delay. Send him a message on his mobile if you can't get hold of him because he'll be able to pick that up even if he's in court."

After ending the call, Peter continued in the same vein focusing upon his rights stating that he would not be answering any questions until Michael London, his solicitor and partner in the firm, London, Harris & Benchley-Smythe, arrived.

"Of course. No problem. I'm going to go outside to make a call myself now, but Constable Cooper will remain in the room with you and Constable Jones will be stationed just outside your door."

Stella was distraught, but did as Peter requested, and then she called Ruth.

"Ruth, Peter has just been arrested! Please can you or George tell me what is happening?"

"Let me ring George and then I'll come straight over."

George explained as much of the situation to Ruth as he was able and told her to assure Stella that they'd be doing their very best to get to the bottom of this as quickly as possible and that if Peter is innocent, he's got nothing to worry about.

Ruth did as George suggested and very soon was sitting in Stella's kitchen helping her to understand what was happening. Stella appeared calmer than she had done over the phone, but, in reality, she was far from calm inside. Her mind kept playing over events that had taken place the day they'd returned from Paris and found Jack in the house. She was not about to share that with Ruth or anyone else because she couldn't explain it herself. Peter had refused to discuss his strange response to what had seemed very much like a threat from Jack when she'd tried to talk about it later. Something was amiss, but surely it didn't involve murder!

Stella seemed lost in her thoughts for a moment, but Ruth, too, was giving thought to other matters, namely, their Mahjong game tomorrow. Obviously, everyone would need to know what had happened and, with that idea, she brought Stella back from her thoughts.

"I know you're not going to play tomorrow. I think Marcus will need you as much as you need him right now, but I do think I should let everyone know about the current situation. Are you comfortable with me doing that, Stella?"

"Yes, no problem, but tomorrow may even be too late as you know how quickly news spreads in a community like ours and how often the stories going around are far from the truth. Maybe you could give each of the girls a call today, so they're the first to hear and know the real situation rather than some gossipy half-truth."

"Yes, of course, I'll do that. Are you going to be all right if I leave you now? You can call me at any time and I'll be straight back if you need me."

"Yes, I'll be fine. I'm sure Marcus will be down soon, I'm sure. He went to his room to call Sebastian as you arrived."

Ruth gave Stella a hug and headed home. She made the three calls as soon as she arrived. Sui Ling, Cathy and Penny were all in agreement that they would find it very hard to concentrate on a game but would still come round to talk.

Michael London wasted no time in getting to the Infirmary after receiving Stella's call.

"I'd like to speak with my client in private, if you don't mind," he said to John Clayton.

"Of course," replied John who signalled to Constable Cooper to leave with him.

"This is a hell of a situation to be in," Peter said to Michael as soon as they were alone.

"All right, fill me in on what's happened so that I know how best to help."

Peter related exactly what had happened stressing that he had nothing to do with the girl's murder.

"I believe you, but we've got to ensure the police believe you too. Why did you refuse the DNA test when that could have exonerated you? You know as well as I do, that they can now force you to have one, so if you're hiding anything, you'd better tell me now."

"I wasn't thinking clearly about the repercussions when George suggested I take the test. I was more concerned about escaping from what it might reveal. I know that's unlike me because I should certainly have known that refusing to take one would make me look guilty and I fully expect them to go ahead and force me to have one now."

"Go on," said Michael.

"This is hard for me to admit, Michael, but I did know Gemma Davies. In fact, I'd been in a relationship with her for almost a year before she died. I'd actually been with her two days beforehand at my flat and knew that they would be able to collect samples of my DNA from her, but I had nothing to do with her death. I did give her the necklace that's just turned up and which has effectively led to my arrest. It was a stupid thing to do from the outset because it's a family heirloom and totally traceable to me."

"Why on earth would you give her a family heirloom?"

"I don't think I gave it to her as much as she wheedled it out of me. I realised I had to go home to pick up some documents one day when the two of us were out for lunch. Stella was away and I knew it would be easy enough to pass Gemma off as a colleague if necessary, but it wasn't, because I didn't see either of the Dorlans."

"Who are the Dorlans?"

"The couple who work for us. Anyway, Gemma saw the necklace in the bathroom and asked if she could have it. I was reluctant as I'd given it to Stella, but Gemma pressed and, figuring that Stella wasn't short of jewellery so would hardly miss it, I agreed when Gemma said that if I loved her, I'd give it to her. I guess I just wanted to keep her happy and maybe look the big man at the same time."

"Given what you've told me, I think you have no choice but to come clean. Assuming the DNA test will reveal your involvement with her anyway, it's better that you admit to the relationship now, rather than waiting until they prove you were connected. We then need to focus upon establishing that you are innocent of her murder."

"Yes, that makes sense."

"Now, what about an alibi for the time of the murder; do you have one?"

"Not really, unless the doormen of my apartment building kept records of everyone's comings and goings because I was in my flat alone that night. There was no reason to come home that week at all because Stella had gone to London to be with her sister for a few days."

"Why wasn't Gemma with you, then?"

"I think she might have told me she was working. We certainly didn't live in each other's pockets."

"Well, I can check out if records were kept by doormen in the building at that time. Is there anything else that I need to know, anything that you think will help your case?"

"I'm not sure about helping my case, but the only other thing I can think of right now is one which might give them a reason to think I'm guilty because she was pregnant!"

"Was it yours?"

"I honestly don't know, but probably yes, and what's worse is that there was a suggestion at the time that her pregnancy could have been the motive for her murder, particularly as there was no evidence of rape. I didn't know she was pregnant, though, until I read about it in the newspapers like everyone else."

"All right, I think it's time for you to give a statement, but I don't think you need me to tell you that it could lead to your being charged with her murder; however, we'll deal with that if and when it happens."

"Yes, I know. My biggest concern at the moment is Stella. Goodness knows what she'll be going through already. I hate what's going to hit her after my confession becomes public knowledge, especially as we've only just turned a corner in our own relationship. Do you think you could arrange for her to visit as I'd rather tell her myself than have her reading about my infidelity in the papers?"

"I can try, but, unless they actually charge you, it's unlikely that she'll be allowed in to see you. The good thing is that you should receive anonymity up until that point, although, of course, there's no guarantee."

"All right, but try your best, please."

Michael nodded before heading to the door and telling the officer standing outside that Peter was ready to make a statement. Once the statement was complete and had been signed by Peter, John informed him that, given the seriousness of the offence for which he'd been arrested, he would be held in custody for the maximum period of ninety-six hours pending further investigations.

The next morning, the ladies arrived at Ruth's one by one, but their usual joy at meeting one another was absent. There was a subdued air as they discussed the situation and their sadness for their friend, Stella, was almost too much to bear.

"I don't believe that he did it," said Cathy. "Do you?" she asked as an open question.

Sui Ling responded by saying, "I'd like to think not, but I'm not going to prejudge as there are stranger things that have happened."

Ruth replied too, "I really hope not and though George is stepping back from the case, I know he will ensure no stone is left unturned to get to the truth. What is important now is for us to take care of Stella. To begin with, we need to keep our own counsel and not say a word to anyone about the case. We may well be asked because not only are we Stella's friends, but everyone knows we've been interested in solving this case."

"Absolutely," said Penny. "We don't want to fuel the fire of gossip, so the best thing we can do is keep mum, especially if the press gets wind of the situation."

"Do you think there's anything we can do to help clear his name?" asked Cathy. "It's such a shame as he should have been coming out of hospital and celebrating his birthday this week and not facing a murder charge. Do you know if he'll be allowed home on bail, Ruth?"

"From what I understand, bail is only an option once a charge has been made, but murder is such a serious charge that there's no guarantee that it would be granted anyway."

"I like your suggestion of us giving her support," said Penny. "I know she has Marcus here, but I'm not sure how long he can stay; besides, we ladies always need girlfriends to talk to when life is challenging."

"How best do you think we can help her, Ruth?" added Sui Ling.

"Well, we certainly need to be there for her if she wants to talk things over, but at the same time we mustn't push her. I think we all need to make contact with her each day, if only by WhatsApp. She needs to know that we're on her side no matter what."

"Do you think it would be a good idea to bake for her, not that I'm a star baker or anything?" asked Cathy.

"Well, you know how she loves her sweet treats. I know she has Brenda to prepare meals for her, but little gifts like that will let her know she's loved and cared for, so I'd say yes, it's a good idea."

The ladies continued brainstorming ways in which to support their friend and this lifted them all from the flatness they'd shared when they'd first come together that morning.

At the same time as the ladies were meeting, Michael was in one of his own. He'd arranged to meet with George Cromwell, whom he'd met on a few occasions when attending events hosted by the Benchley-Smythes.

"Thank you for seeing me at such short notice, George. How are you?"

"I'm good. It's a pleasure to see you again, Michael, but I'm sure you've not come by to ask after my welfare. I understand you're acting on behalf of Peter."

"I am, yes, and my visit is connected with the case because I want to talk about how best to help Peter at this stage. His greatest concern right now is not for himself but for Stella. He doesn't want her to find out about his affair with Gemma Davies on the grapevine or via the press. Ideally, he'd like to tell her himself, but, of course, he knows that no visitors are allowed between the arrest and charge period. I realise that you're not personally handling the case and so may not feel able to intervene and give any special dispensations, so I've already considered alternative options and think that if Peter can't have a visit, then someone who cares about Stella should break the news to her. Now, I'd do it myself, but not being married, I'm probably not be the best person to offer comfort afterwards, so I thought that perhaps you and Ruth might consider breaking the news to her as you're such good friends."

"Well, you're right on both counts. I'm not going to intervene because I don't want to be seen to be giving favours to friends. I think, because of my role in the force, it's actually best that I maintain a distance from them for the time being. However, there's no reason why Ruth can't go with you. I don't want her to feel that I'm pressuring her in any way, so I'm going to suggest that you just give her a call and invite her yourself. To be honest, I'm pretty sure she'll say yes because she's already been thinking of ways to support Stella."

"That sounds like a good plan. I'll give her a call and see if she could actually go over with me today. The sooner this is done the better. Thank you, George."

"Yes, do that, I know she's with the Mahjong group right now, but they're usually finished by mid-afternoon, so hopefully she'll be able to go with you today."

Chapter 17

The Charge

"Ding-dong!"

Stella's swirling thoughts, which had been plaguing her since Peter's arrest, were interrupted by the sound of the doorbell, and she quickly headed to the front door.

"Oh, I'm surprised to see you two visiting me together. I'm sorry, look at me. I'm being so rude. Please come in," said Stella opening the door a little wider.

"Thank you," Ruth responded.

Once inside, Stella continued, "Did you two actually come together or just land upon my doorstep at the same time?"

"We actually did come together," said Ruth, "because Michael has some news that Peter wants him to share with you and he felt it would be good for me to be here just as a friend."

"Oh, that sounds ominous; I'm not sure I want to hear what you've got to say," said Stella, her expression unable to hide the fear of what might be coming next.

"Shall I make us all a hot drink first?" offered Ruth.

"No, let's get this over with," Stella urged. "I might not

like what I'm going to hear, but I hate living in limbo!"

Michael began and didn't stop until he'd explained the whole situation to Stella. Despite tears that had so obviously welled up and looked ready to flow, she sat still, not uttering a word. Ruth simply put a comforting hand on Stella's arm which seemed to draw Stella out as she then responded.

"I don't know what to say or what to think. I know Peter's shortcomings better than anyone and, though I'd like to say the affair comes as a surprise, it doesn't, but, despite this, I find it hard to believe that he's a murderer."

Michael responded, "I agree with you, Stella. Peter may not have been the most faithful of men, but murder, well that's in a different league altogether. I have to admit though that things don't look good for him at this point."

"Where's Marcus?" Ruth asked. "Do you think he should be here too Stella?"

"He went out to get a few bits and bobs as soon as we got back from the hospital, but only to the village. Do you think I should call him?"

Michael answered, "Yes, if you want me to explain the situation to him too. If he's able to get back quickly, it will certainly give him the chance to ask any questions he might have."

Stella tried calling several times over the next ten minutes, but to no avail.

"I'm sorry, he's probably talking to Sebastian. He's usually quite short and to the point when on a call, but not when he's chatting to Sebastian," she explained.

"No worries, just tell him that he can give me a call at any time if he feels the need."

Michael said his farewells as Ruth and Stella headed to the kitchen, where they found Brenda already making a pot of tea. "I hope you don't mind, but I overheard everything that Peter's partner said. I'm sure he didn't do it. They're sure to discover that."

"I wish I was as confident as you sound," Stella replied. "Oh, Ruth, whatever am I supposed to do now? I can't visit him or do anything practical to help. I think I'm going to go crazy as my mind was whirling even before I knew about the affair. On the one hand, I could kill Peter myself for bringing this on the family, but on the other I don't want him blamed for something he didn't do, if we're right and he didn't do it. I seriously don't know what to think now. What am I to do?"

"At this stage, I think we have no option but to sit tight and trust the system. Besides, George is in overall charge of the case and he cares for you both, so he's going to leave no stone unturned in getting to the bottom of this for both your sakes as well as for Gemma's family. He's already going through the case files with a fine-tooth comb to see if he can unearth anything that wasn't spotted by those working on it at the time. In the meantime, you have me and everyone in our lovely Mahjong group to lean on. How about I arrange an impromptu game tomorrow so that you can see them all?

Focusing your mind on a game may give you an emotional break too. What do you think?"

"Oh, I don't know if I could focus on a game, but, yes, I'd love to see them and try. I definitely need company, supportive company that is. In fact, let me host the game and I can do a little baking this afternoon to give me something practical to do."

"All right, I'll let everyone know," said Ruth and I'll be here early in case you need a little support before everyone arrives. Will you be all right if I leave now?"

"Yes, of course, I've got Brenda here and Marcus will no doubt be back before too long. I'll see you tomorrow."

At that, Ruth left, but it was not the end of the conversation as far as Stella was concerned because once they were alone, she explained the situation to Brenda. Then, for the first time, they talked about the strange interaction they'd both witnessed between Peter and Jack when Stella and Peter had returned home from Paris, but still neither of them could make any sense of it.

As soon as Brenda got home to the cottage, she shared everything with Eric and both agreed they had to make a call.

"Jack, it's me, mum. Please can you come over as soon as possible because your dad and I have something important we need to talk to you about."

"Sure, I'll come over this weekend. I was going to ask you for a bit of a loan anyway. I just need a hundred to tide me over so it will give me a chance to pick up the cash."

Brenda's disappointment could be seen on her face and Eric was not slow to see this or to ask her what Jack had said as soon as the call ended. Nor was he surprised when he heard that Jack was after money.

On Wednesday morning, the first thing Stella received from each of the ladies when they arrived for the added extra Mahjong session was a great big hug.

"Have there been any developments since yesterday, Stella?" asked Sui Ling.

"No, I've not heard anything more," replied Stella.

"Dan and I are shocked to the core and convinced they have not got their man," added Cathy.

Ruth quickly interjected. "Let's remember that this is just normal police procedure designed to get to the truth. Being under arrest doesn't mean that Peter is guilty. Obviously, it means there is some evidence that points to him, but it also gives him an opportunity to prove his innocence and clear his name."

"Is there anything we can do to help at this stage, Ruth?" asked Penny.

"To be honest not that I can think of as the matter is now firmly back in the hands of the police. The best thing we can do is to leave them to get on with their job while we look after Stella."

"Yes, I agree," said Sui Ling, "and on that note, let's get a game going. I think we should play the Western game so that we need to get our thinking caps on."

"Oh no, I didn't bring my book. Can I borrow one as there's no way I can remember all the hands I will have to choose from?" asked Cathy.

"Yes, you can use mine," offered Ruth. "I'm going to put the kettle on and make us some hot drinks. Stella, maybe you can help Sui Ling set everything up."

Happy to have something to do that would relieve her torment, Stella gladly did as Ruth asked and, before long, the first game was underway. Ruth served everyone with a drink and a biscuit on the side and then sat down beside Cathy ready to give her guidance if needed.

"I'm East Wind," said Cathy excitedly after drawing her tile. She then threw the dice. "Six," she said and then she began counting which led to the wall being broken on the West side.

Happily, for Stella, the hours whizzed by and it was a day that gave her some pleasure despite the dark time she was living through. Needless to say, everyone else enjoyed the day too, primarily because they could see Stella smiling and enjoying the games. They played well into the afternoon and so focused were they, both before and after lunch, that, at times, the only sounds that could be heard were game oriented: birds twittering, tile names being spoken as they were being discarded and, of course, the words 'Pung', 'Kong', 'Chow', 'fishing' and 'Mahjong' breaking the silence as everyone concentrated hard on trying to win. Fortunately, success greeted them all as everyone won at least two games with some winning even more. Ruth and Cathy were among the big winners of the day as playing together, they not only won the most games, but they won one game with the most difficult hand that Cathy had ever played: 'Plucking the Moon from the Bottom of the Sea'.

Alas, the pleasure ended in one fell swoop less than an hour after the Mahjong ladies had left. Michael called to say that she and Marcus were now free to visit Peter this evening, but the words that followed gave her no pleasure whatsoever because he went on to say that Peter had now been charged with Gemma's murder and was being remanded in custody. He also told her that Peter would be transferred to prison once his doctor deemed him fit to be moved.

Two hours later, Marcus ushered Stella past the police guard and into Peter's hospital room saying that he would go and get drinks, but it was simply a way of giving his parents some time alone together.

Emotions ran high in both Peter and Stella. Peter was genuinely heartbroken when he saw the pain on Stella's face. Even he knew that his apologies could not put things right, but he continued apologising regardless. At the same time, he kept assuring Stella that he was innocent of the girl's murder. The tears that had constantly been threatening to fall from Stella's eyes now fell freely as she found it difficult to process all the mixed emotions she was feeling inside. Love, anger, hate, fear and compassion were all intermingled. Nevertheless, the one coherent sentence that she did manage to utter was that she believed him to be innocent of the murder and that they would work the rest out together. At this, Peter's love for Stella peaked to such a level that he'd never experienced before and he, too, dissolved into tears.

"I know I've been worse than a fool and I don't deserve you or Marcus, but, when I'm free, I'm going to spend the rest of my life making it up to you both."

They hugged and when Marcus arrived, the three of them hugged like they'd never done before.

The following day, shortly after Stella had arrived home from a morning visit with Peter, Michael called to let her know that he'd just been informed that Peter would remain in custody in his hospital room rather than being transferred to prison. He also told her that a court date had been set for the latest possible date, in four weeks, to give him additional time to recover. Once again, Michael assured Stella that he would be doing his very best to secure Peter's release and that she must ring him without delay if she had any questions or thought of anything that would help Peter's case. At this, her mind flew straight back to the strange interchange that she and Brenda had witnessed in January. She related the whole story to Michael on the phone and asked him to discuss it with Peter.

"I'm heading over there now. Can you give me the next few hours alone with him so that we can discuss this and begin preparations for the hearing?"

"Don't worry, I've no plans to go back today. Marcus is flying back to Paris tonight and we're having an early dinner together before he leaves."

Once alone with Peter in his hospital room, Michael raised the interchange that Stella had reported.

"Well, I've got nothing to hide now and, though I can't see how it helps my case, I'm happy to share with you," said Peter. "Jack is just a complete waster who has been holding a gun to my head for years. When he was nineteen, I caught him red-handed stealing my Rolex watch, but, in all honesty, he's been a problem for everyone connected with him for as long as I can remember, especially for Brenda and Eric who have suffered at his hands for years. It started with truancy in junior school and a whole range of petty crimes followed. It was hardly surprising when he started taking drugs too. He's never been able to hold down a job for more than a few weeks and, instead, has spent much of his time hanging around with every ne'er-do-well in the vicinity.

"When I caught him with my Rolex in hand, I acted as anyone would who'd found themselves being robbed and told Jack to put it down and get the hell out of my house. I told him I'd every intention of calling the police, but he went on to say, 'If you report me, I'll tell everyone about the flat you keep in that sweet little street in Leeds, where you have visits from whoever is the latest in your string of affairs.'

"I was taken aback and halted in my steps by his words. I'd no idea Jack knew about my indiscretions; in fact, as far as I was concerned, no one did. I'd been at pains to keep that side of my life discreet and this was not a revelation that I wanted airing. I was stunned into silence, but Jack, who was high on some drug or other then said, 'I'm going to walk out of here with this watch and you're not going to stop me or say a word to anyone unless you want me to air your dirty linen in public.' To be honest Jack's demeanour was so menacing that I just let him walk away with the watch hoping that would be the end of it. Stupid, really. because he's been **blackmailing me on and off for twenty years**, but only for small sums of cash when visiting his parents, which to be honest he only ever bothers to do when he wants something from them. I guess he didn't want to push his luck too far."

"Do you think he could be capable of murder?" asked Michael.

"Not really. I think he's just a petty criminal with an eye to the main chance."

Chapter 18

The Attack

Early on Friday morning, Brenda was at home baking in readiness for the weekend when Jack walked in making her jump.

"Oh, my goodness, I didn't expect you today. I thought you'd be arriving tomorrow."

"I know, but I didn't feel like work today, so I'm pulling a sickie. I actually think I'm going to be fired when I go back anyway, but who cares. So, what's so important that you wanted me to come over?"

His words were slurred as if he'd been drinking, but Brenda knew the signs all too well and guessed that even if he had been drinking, he was probably also high on some drug or other.

She urged him to sit down and handing him a glass of cold water, said, "Here, sip this and I'll get some peanuts for you to snack on. How are you feeling? I'm amazed you could even drive in this state."

"I'm great; in fact, better than great. I'm on top of the world!"

Upon hearing Jack's overly loud voice, Eric came downstairs, but he took one look at his son, then rolling his eyes said almost under his breath, "He'll never change!"

"Dad, it's great to see you. I've got an amazing business idea. I'm going to make us all rich."

"What is it this time, Jack?" asked Eric with a sigh.

"Stan and I are going to buy a van and turn it into a mobile cinema and we'll show drive-in movies every night in fields outside towns and villages. This is a winner for sure. We just need to get the money together to buy the van and then fit it out. I thought you and mum might like to buy some shares."

"I don't think so, son. We don't have the money to invest in anything."

Jack was undeterred. He raved about his idea and what he would do when he was 'crazy rich' as he called it. He talked almost non-stop for close to two hours before they sensed he was starting to show signs of coming down. Brenda decided this was the right time to let him know what had been happening at the Manor because she knew him of old and realised that he could possibly take another shot of whatever poison he was on if he started to feel low.

"Jack, I hope it all works out for you, but right now, we've got important things to discuss because Peter is in serious trouble. He's been arrested for the murder of that girl who was killed in Bentham Woods. We have to speak up and share that she was here at the house the day before she was found dead. It's evidence that could help Peter and Stella. Your dad and I think we should call the police and ask them to come over so that the three of us can all give a statement together."

"What! Are you out of your minds?" he shouted. "They're going to think I killed her if we do that, especially as I left here shortly after she did. I'm not going to go along with that hair-brained scheme."

"But you're not the murderer, so you'll be cleared even if you do become a suspect. We have to help the family; we can't let them suffer in this way."

"Your mum is right, son. We must do the right thing now that Peter has been charged with a murder that we don't believe he committed."

"What makes you think he didn't do it?" Jack snapped.

"You know as well as we do that Peter was in Leeds when she turned up here," said Eric, "and if we can testify to that fact, it's bound to help his case."

"No! I'm not getting dragged into this," Jack shouted, "and I'm not going to let either of you involve me. No way."

His anger was now beginning to turn into rage and Eric was trying to calm him down. Nevertheless, undeterred, Brenda picked up her phone because with or without Jack's support, she was going to do what she and Eric believed to be the right thing. She knew they had to ensure Peter didn't take the blame for something he didn't do. However, just as she was about to make the call, she felt a searing pain in her back followed by a second, which instantly brought her to her knees. She then collapsed onto the floor managing to turn her head just in time to see Eric moving towards her and Jack plunging the kitchen knife into his stomach. As she passed out, her heart went out to Eric who she instinctively knew had been coming to her aid.

Jack, even in his stupefied state, could hardly believe what he'd just done, but, seeing the knife in his hands and blood splattered everywhere, he made the decision to run. He swiftly headed out of the cottage, got into his somewhat battered car and raced away from the scene.

Stella, who by this time was concerned that the usually punctual Brenda hadn't turned up for work at 10 a.m., decided to take a stroll over to the cottage to find out if everything was all right. She was just in time to see a car disappearing out of sight. She saw the dust flying and knew it was travelling far too fast for the dirt road. Beginning to feel very uneasy, she hurried a little faster towards the cottage.

Upon arrival, she found the door wide open, which again was very strange, but what she saw inside horrified her so much that she heaved and had to step back out into the fresh air where she actually vomited. She, too, wanted to run away, although she knew that she couldn't.

Composing herself, she went back inside speaking both of their names out loud. Eric didn't make a sound, but a moan came from Brenda to which Stella quickly responded. Bending down by her side, Stella realised that Brenda was not only her long-term housekeeper but also a beloved friend. Brenda was trying to speak, but Stella said, "Hush, don't try to talk, just save your energy, I'm going to ring for help."

As soon as Stella put the mobile back in her pocket, she assured Brenda that an ambulance was on its way. Brenda tried to speak again, but this time, Stella bent to listen; however, the only word she could catch was 'Jack'.

Stella's mind raced, surely Brenda wasn't trying to say that Jack was responsible. Even he would not be capable of this massacre. He was just a spoilt, lazy, good-for-nothing son, but, again, she heard Brenda utter his name. Was Brenda really trying to say Jack had done this or was she just wanting Stella to call Jack for her? She could see Brenda's mobile on the floor where she would certainly be able to find Jack's number, but her instinct told her not to touch it or anything else. Instead, she kept a comforting hand on Brenda's shoulder uttering words of reassurance until she realised Brenda was no longer conscious. She then went to check on Eric, who she was devastated to find was already dead.

Stella decided to call Ruth as she waited in the now eerily silent cottage. Ruth said she'd contact George immediately and come over herself. However, by the time Ruth spoke to George, he was aware of the situation and already on his way.

The ambulance arrived and both Eric and Brenda were carried out of the cottage on stretchers with Eric's head completely covered confirming what Stella already knew to be true.

George and Ruth arrived at the cottage almost at the same time, but George suggested they go back to Stella's to talk while the police in attendance set about sealing off the cottage in readiness for the crime scene investigation team's arrival.

Once in Stella's home, George asked her what had happened.

"I really don't know. I saw a car driving away as I neared the cottage, but I couldn't identify it. The only thing I can say for sure was that it was travelling far too fast on the dirt road."

"Tell me what you saw once you arrived at the cottage," George continued.

Stella told him everything in as much detail as she could, including the fact that Brenda had mouthed the name 'Jack' twice. "Maybe we should call him to let him know what's happened because he is their son after all. I don't actually know his number, but it will certainly be in Brenda's phone which was on the floor not far from her hand."

"Don't worry, we'll be sure to make contact with him. I need to head back to the cottage now. Are you able to stay here with Stella, Ruth, or do you want me to get one of the policewomen to come over?"

"No, don't do that; I'll stay. Maybe Stella can come and spend a few days with us, at least until Marcus gets back."

"That sounds like a good idea," George said and turning to Stella, he continued, "Please know that I'd be just as happy as Ruth for you to come and stay with us. It will give us both peace of mind to know that you're not alone here."

"Thank you both," Stella replied. "I'd like to do that, but, please, could I go and have a shower now as I feel so unclean after being in the cottage. I can still smell the blood."

"Of course," said Ruth, "and as soon as you're ready, I can help you pack a bag and head on over to our place."

George went back to the cottage, but he'd no sooner arrived than he was told that the ambulance driver taking Brenda and Eric to the hospital had spotted an upturned car in the wooded area less than two miles from the cottage. Given Brenda's condition, it wasn't possible for them to stop to check it out, but they'd immediately radioed in and George was told that two officers had already left the cottage and were on their way to the scene of the crash and that another car in the vicinity was also on its way there.

George jumped into his own car and headed up the road towards the crash site wondering how he could possibly have missed seeing it himself, but, once he arrived, he realised that the car was hidden from view as it had veered off the road into bushes not stopping until it had hit a tree and overturned about fifty yards in. He figured that the ambulance driver must have been seated high enough in his cab to see over the bushes lining the edge of the road.

As George pulled to a stop behind two police cars, he could hear the sirens of an approaching ambulance. An officer standing by the side of the road informed him that the driver had already been identified from his driving licence as Jack Dorlan. George then headed over to Jack's car with the paramedics who by this time had arrived. The car had obviously lost its battle against an old oak tree and would no doubt be classed as a 'write-off'. Together the two paramedics carefully extracted Jack from the wreckage and began their medical examination and though he was unconscious, the medical assessment revealed his injuries to be superficial.

Meanwhile, one of the officers at the scene who had been trying to confirm that Jack was the owner of the vehicle discovered that the registration number was listed on the Police National Database as stolen.

By this time, Jack was being transferred into the ambulance, but, as a suspected car thief and possible killer, a police car was not only assigned to accompany the ambulance, but one officer also travelled inside the ambulance with him.

George left and after a short visit back to the cottage to liaise with the officers in attendance there, he headed home and told Stella and Ruth what had transpired.

"We know it's Jack Dorlan and the evidence from the scene indicates that he was driving at speed when his car veered off the road, but although he's unconscious, it seems there are no serious injuries. I've asked to be kept informed and they will let me know as soon as he comes round and is considered fit to be interviewed."

"What about Brenda?" asked Stella.

"She's going to be all right as the knife didn't penetrate any vital organs. She's been very lucky; hopefully, we should be able to talk to her tomorrow because I'm told she's already coming round, but, of course, the bad news about Eric has still to be broken to her. We have a policewoman standing by and liaising with the doctor in order to decide when to break the news."

"Oh, what a relief to know she's going to be all right. Will she be allowed visitors do you think?" asked Stella. "She's going to need a lot of support, especially after she's been told about Eric."

"I don't see any reason why not, but perhaps it's best to wait and see how she is after she receives the news and has been interviewed."

The following morning, George arrived at the hospital where he was greeted by WPC Amanda Drake. She told him that Brenda was fully conscious and quite coherent. She also said she'd liaised with the doctor who had agreed to be with her when she broke the news about Eric so that he could explain about the injuries if Brenda wanted to know.

"I'm just waiting for him to arrive now," she explained.

"That's good," said George. "I'll also come in with you so that I can talk to her straight afterwards if I think she's up to it."

"Yes, sir, and, if I may, I'll stay beside her as you ask the questions to provide some female support if she needs comforting."

"Of, course. All right, I'm going to grab a coffee while we wait for the doctor to arrive. Can I get you one?"

"No, thank you, sir, I had a drink not too long ago."

"Okay, I'll be back in a few minutes."

By the time George got back, the doctor had arrived and all three went in to see Brenda together. Having known her for years, George naturally greeted her like an old friend. He then introduced WPC Drake as Amanda, explaining that they'd got some news that she was going to share. Then, in the most, gentle of ways, Amanda broke the news of Eric's death. Brenda's tears began to fall upon hearing the news and she wept for some time with Amanda simply holding her hands and passing tissues as needed. All three of them remained silent allowing Brenda to grieve until she herself regained some composure. At that point, she explained that she could remember every detail of the attack and had already feared that Eric had not survived.

"I know it won't be easy, Brenda, but we need to find out who did this to you and why. Could you share with me all the details that you remember, in your own time, of course?"

"I know who did it. It was Jack, our son, and maybe I know why, though I'm sure if he hadn't been high on drugs, he'd never have done this. I don't know how he's going to live with himself when he realises what he's done."

Chapter 19

The Sentence

"Why do you think he did it, Brenda?"

"I know that too. It was because of what we wanted him to do, but neither of us could ever have imagined he would hurt us."

"Please go on," encouraged George.

"Well, I called and asked Jack to come over after Peter was charged with that girl's murder because the three of us have information that we'd never spoken of at the time. Eric and I had already decided that we needed to share it with you to help Peter clear his name and we wanted Jack to agree, but he refused saying it would make him a suspect. I tried to tell him he would be cleared even if he did become a suspect, but he was adamant that we keep it to ourselves, but I just couldn't. It was as I made a move to make a call that he attacked, first me and then Eric."

"Could you share that information with me now?" George asked.

"Yes, of course. We never told anyone, but the girl, Gemma Davies, came to Hazelby Manor the day before her body was found, so probably on the very day she was murdered. Actually, it was an unusual day all round because all three of us, Jack, Eric and I, were in the Manor having words at the time. Jack knew that he was never to go into Peter's and Stella's home, but I caught him in Peter's dressing room rifling through his belongings. Fortunately, Eric was tending to the plants in the kitchen garden at the time, so I quickly went down to ask him to go and sort Jack out, but by the time we both got upstairs, Jack was walking out of the dressing room with a pair of gold cufflinks. Eric told him to put them back, but Jack refused saying that Peter would give him money if he was there, so he was taking the cufflinks to sell as he needed to raise some cash. We asked him why on earth Peter would give him money and all that Jack would say is that it was a private arrangement. I asked him to tell me what he meant by that, but that's when I heard the front doorbell ring."

George could see that Brenda was wilting, so he asked if she was feeling well enough to continue.

"I'm sorry, but I am actually feeling quite unwell. Please, could I have a glass of water and a bit of a rest?"

"Of course, I'll leave you to get some rest and ask a nurse to bring you a drink. I'll also leave Amanda here, so just let her know when you feel ready to continue and she'll give me a call."

"Thank you," she said gratefully.

Two hours later, George received a call from Amanda telling him that Brenda felt ready to talk again, so he headed straight back to the hospital.

After greeting Brenda and hearing from her own lips that she felt well enough to continue the interview, George went straight back into interview mode.

"So, the last thing you told me was that you heard the doorbell ringing, Brenda. Can you pick up from that point?"

"Yes, the doorbell silenced all of us and I hurried downstairs and when I opened the door, this girl, who I'd never seen before, just pushed straight past me asking to see Mrs. Benchley-Smythe. I told her she was not at home, that I was the housekeeper and she'd better leave. She said she wasn't going anywhere and that she and Peter were in love and were having a baby together. She also said it wouldn't be long before she became Mrs. Benchley-Smythe and I'd be working for her. She even had the cheek to stand there and tell me that when she was the Lady of the Manor there'd be no future for me if I didn't start treating her with respect."

After a brief break when she closed her eyes, she continued, "That's when I realised she was wearing Stella's necklace, a valuable one that had been missing for months. I knew then that something was amiss, and I actually began to think that there might be some truth in this girl's story, not least because I knew Peter had had an eye for the ladies ever since he was a young man. To be honest though, we always thought he just liked to flirt and that was as far as it went but seeing the necklace around her neck made me feel very uneasy."

"What happened next?" George prompted.

"Well, I managed to calm the girl down and asked Eric to bring some tea so that we could talk. She told me her name was Gemma and that she and Peter had been in a relationship for the past year and that he planned to divorce his wife and marry her. But then she said she'd been trying to ring him for the last two days, but he hadn't answered her calls. It all sounded very strange. Anyway, she went on to tell me that she'd decided to come to the house to tell his wife she was pregnant to force his hand. She was in an emotional state, but, after a little while, I managed to convince her that it would be better for her to go home because Peter wouldn't be back for a few days at the earliest and Stella was in London visiting her sister for the whole week. She agreed after I promised to call and let her know when Peter returned; I said this more to get rid of her than anything else."

"So, she left at that point?" asked George.

"Yes, and very shortly afterwards Jack said he was leaving too; in fact, within half an hour he'd gone. Sadly, I discovered later that the cufflinks were gone too. I called him straight away to try and convince him to return them, but he didn't answer my call. I guessed it would probably be too late to get them back from him, but, as he would be coming back to the house the following day, I thought I could at least try to convince him to return them then."

"So, he left the house very soon after Gemma? Do you suppose he caught up with her on the road? Is he a fast driver?" asked George.

"Yes, he's a fast driver, but he said he'd not seen her on the road when we asked him after she'd been found dead the next day."

"Did he say anything else?"

"Well, he was the one who asked us not to say anything about her coming to the Manor because he thought the timing could make it look as though he'd had something to do with it. We knew it wouldn't look good for him, especially as he had a criminal record for petty offences, so Eric and I agreed to keep silent for his sake."

"You said you knew he'd be back the following day; why would he be returning?"

"Oh, because he had to borrow Peter's car. Not that Eric had given him permission, but he demanded it saying he needed to get back to Leeds to bring a battery back for his own car, which wouldn't start, and, when Jack is using, you know, taking drugs, you just don't argue too much with him."

"So, what type of car did Peter have at the time?"

"It was a Range Rover. In fact, like every other man in the village who owned one at the time, Peter was questioned."

"So, you're telling me that your son was driving a Range Rover when he left shortly after Gemma?"

"Yes."

"Did it ever cross your mind that he might be the killer knowing that he'd been driving Peter's car on the day she was killed?"

"Oh, no, he might not have been the best son in the world, but we never believed for a single minute that he did it."

"Now Brenda, I'm sure you know that withholding evidence is an offence. I need you to think carefully and tell me if there's anything else I need to know."

"No there's nothing else to tell, but I am sorry. We really didn't think we were doing anything wrong. It just seemed sensible not to involve Jack when we knew he would never do such a thing."

"All right, we'll leave it there for now, Brenda, and talk about the situation again later as I can see you need another rest. In the meantime, if anything comes to mind that you think I ought to know, just press your call button and let one of the nurses know you need to speak to the officer, who will be on duty outside your room tonight."

"Amanda, why don't you head off home now; you've had a couple of very full days."

"Thank you, sir, just let me know if you need me before tomorrow at nine."

After leaving Brenda's room, George went to the ward where Jack was being held and asked to speak to someone who could give information about the medical fitness of Jack to be questioned. The doctor on duty said that in his opinion Jack was already fit enough to be interviewed, so George immediately set things in motion assigning two officers to begin the process that very afternoon. As he headed back to the office to catch up on his own paperwork, George called Ruth to let her know he'd be home for dinner at the usual time.

The minute he walked in the door, Ruth and Stella started firing questions at him. "How is Brenda?" Ruth asked quickly followed by Stella asking, "When can I visit?"

"Okay, okay, ladies, give me a minute to catch my breath."

After removing his coat, he responded. "Right, you'll be happy to know that Brenda's doing well, Ruth, and you'll be pleased to know that you can visit her tomorrow, Stella. She's been very helpful today, but I can't go into detail yet, other than to say she's identified Jack as the attacker."

"My goodness. How dreadful; their own son!" said Ruth.

"I honestly don't know how she's ever going to get over this," added Stella. "She dotes on him, even though he's never been anything but trouble, and now she's not even got Eric! I'll go first thing in the morning."

The next day both George and Stella left the house at the same time and headed in the same direction, but, once inside the hospital, they went in opposite directions.

"Oh, Brenda, I'm so sorry," Stella said as soon as she walked into Brenda's room, but Brenda gave no response;

she just burst into tears at the sight of Stella, who immediately put her arms around her and hugged her tightly. The two remained this way until Brenda's tears subsided.

The scene was very different in Jack's room. George had entered during a session of questioning, but all he could hear was 'No comment' as Jack's response to every question. The legal representative who had been assigned to Jack was sitting by his bed, but, in the fifteen minutes George had been standing at the back of the room, he did not hear him utter a single word. At this point, George decided to intervene.

"Look, Jack, we already know that you attacked your parents resulting in the death of your father. Fortunately, your mother survived and she has already identified you as their attacker. We're going to be charging you with one count of murder and one of attempted murder as well as being in possession of a stolen vehicle, but I want to raise another issue now because I have reason to believe you are also responsible for the murder of Gemma Davies. Your mother has told me about the day Gemma Davies came to Hazelby Manor and she also told me that you left shortly after Gemma. She also mentioned that you left in Peter Benchley-Smythe's Range Rover."

Jack demeanor didn't change nor did he respond.

"I can tell you now, Jack, that once you are charged, we're going to be doing a DNA test that I believe will confirm you are guilty of Gemma's murder. Now, given all that I have said, I want you to think seriously about your plea because if you deny the charges and are found guilty through witness accounts and DNA results, your sentence is more than likely going to reflect your unwillingness to cooperate. However, if you decide not to waste any more police time and come clean, this will be taken into consideration by the judge when he comes to deciding on the severity of your sentence."

At this, Jack's lawyer spoke for the first time in George's presence. He simply asked if he could have time alone with his client. George and the two officers that had been questioning Jack all left the room. Within half an hour, Jack's lawyer came out of the room and confirmed that Jack was now prepared to make a statement.

As soon as the statement had been signed, George went directly to see Peter.

"Good news, old boy, you're off the hook. Jack Dorlan has just confessed to the murder of Gemma Davies. As soon as you're fit and well, you can go home. Off the record my friend, I would say this, you've got a lot of making up to do as far as your family is concerned and you want to thank your lucky stars that Stella and Marcus have been so supportive and steadfast in their belief that you were innocent."

"I've never received better news, and I intend to spend the rest of my life making it up to both of them because you're absolutely right. Thank you for letting me know so quickly. Now, I guess I don't have to ask you if I can make a call," he said with a smile.

George patted Peter on the shoulder and then headed out feeling very satisfied that justice was going to be done.

"Hi, Ruth," George said when she answered his call. "We've got our man!"

After briefly telling her what had transpired, Ruth responded by saying, "Oh, that's wonderful news! I'm going to call the girls now and let them know."

On the day that Jack appeared in court, Ruth, Stella, Sui Ling, Penny and Cathy were all in attendance. Thankfully, the trial didn't take long due to Jack's guilty plea. That day they discovered what George had known since Jack's confession, but had withheld, so as not to compromise the case in any way.

Jack had left Hazelby Manor just thirty minutes after Gemma Davies. He'd had every intention of heading straight back to Leeds to pick up the spare battery that was charging in his flat and returning the following day to get his own car up and running again. However, while driving along the road taking him through Bentham Woods, he'd spotted a car parked by the side of the road. It had struck him as somewhat strange at the time, as it was a pretty lonely stretch of road, but, as he got closer, he realised it was the Mazda 3 that Gemma had driven away from Hazelby Manor in not too long ago.

He pulled to a stop behind her and, by the time he'd opened his door, she was already heading towards him relief evident on her face. She told him she'd got a flat tyre and he offered to help, but he was already thinking what an ideal situation he was in to keep his meal ticket intact. His biggest concern when he'd heard Gemma's story was that he'd no longer have a hold over Peter and be able to maintain the steady stream of blackmail income he'd managed to create for himself.

With Gemma by his side, he unlocked the boot and lifted out the floor panel to reveal the spare wheel. He reached for the wheel brace at the left-hand side of the compartment with his right hand and then, seizing the opportunity, he lifted it out, turned and brought it down on her head. She'd immediately fallen backwards tripping over the kerb and falling onto the grass, but that didn't stop Jack who then brought the wheel brace down upon her head three more times. He figured his financial concerns were no more when he saw her lying motionless in a pool of blood. However, he knew he still had to deal with her body and her car, so he went back to the Range Rover and put on the driving gloves he'd seen in the console and then dragged her body into the woodland. He pushed it under bushes sufficiently far from the road so as not to be easily found. He then drove her car into the woodland until it, too, was hidden from the road.

He'd then returned to the Range Rover, removed the gloves and stuffed them into his pocket before getting back in and driving away. The next day, he'd returned a pristine freshly valeted Range Rover back to Hazelby Manor.

His sentence came as no surprise to anyone in the court that day. No one would have anything to fear from Jack Dorlan for a very long time to come, for the mandatory life-sentence handed down came with a ruling that he must serve a minimum of twenty-five years before becoming eligible for parole.

Chapter 20

The Mahjong Maramas

"Oh, my goodness, look at all of this mail," said Ruth when she opened the bag that George had just handed to her.

The ladies were equally astonished when they arrived to play Mahjong just one week after the trial. "Where did it all come from?" Stella asked when she saw the mailbag full of letters and printed emails sitting on Ruth's kitchen table.

"Well, George brought the bag home after he was contacted by the editor of the Post. It seems letters and emails have been pouring into newspaper offices and television studios ever since our story broke. Some of them have been addressed very interestingly to names such as 'The Mahjong Ladies', 'The Yorkshire Cold Case Detectives' and 'The Housewife Sleuths' to name just a few."

"What do they want? Why would so many people want to get in touch with us?" asked Cathy.

Ruth answered, "Well, from those I've read, most are from people who want us to help them find missing family members or hunt down the killers of their loved ones. Basically, we're being asked to get involved in unresolved cases and some ongoing cases; a number of them have even come from overseas!"

"Well," Penny said, "all of the papers and news reports have been saying what a great job we did. Maybe it's only to be expected. There must be many frustrated people out there who don't know where to turn, particularly when cases go cold, but is this something we all want to continue doing?"

"Well, if we do," Sui Ling chipped in, "let me tell you about a case that my daughter, Candy, has suggested we might like to become involved in for it seems to be confounding everyone at her university in Scotland. It's certainly not gone cold yet, but the police are at a loss to even know if there's been a murder let alone who might be responsible. A professor has gone missing under strange circumstances and everyone in the Philosophy Department is under suspicion. On top of that, it seems staff members are all afraid that they might be next!"

"Actually, I quite like the idea of getting my teeth into another case," said Penny. "What about you, girls?"

"I'm in," said Stella. "I particularly like the idea of clearing the names of innocent people."

"Me too," agreed Ruth, "but let's read through the rest of the letters and emails because we should at least reply to everyone and we may also identify cases where we could really be of help, if not now, certainly in the future."

"Oh, ladies, I'm afraid you're going to have to count me out for the time being," said Cathy, patting her bump, "but I do have a great name for us."

"Really? I'd not even thought about a name," said Ruth.

"What is it?"

"The Mahjong Maramas!"

"Where did that spring from?" asked Sui Ling.

"Well," said Cathy, "I came across the word 'Maramas' not too long ago in a book set in the South Pacific and loved it from the very first minute. It rolls off the tongue and one of its meanings is 'light'. What better name could we have as we aim to shine a light in dark places?"

The Mahjong Maramas! All agreed it was the name for them!

Glossary of Terms

Mahjong Terminology

Chow: A run of three tiles of the same suit

Fishing: The call a player needs to make when only one tile away from achieving Mahjong.

Kong: A set of four identical tiles

Pung: A set of three identical tiles

Plucking the Moon from the Bottom of the Sea: The 'moon' is the 1 of Circles and Mahjong is achieved by a player who upon drawing the last tile from the wall finds that it is the 'moon' which also allows the player to call Mahjong.

Chinese Food Items

Char Siu Bao: Steamed buns stuffed with barbecued pork

Har Gau: Translucent shrimp dumplings

Nian Gao: glutinous brown sugar cake wrapped in pastry and deep fried shrimp and pork filling sticking out over the top.

Lo Mai Gai: Sticky rice and meats wrapped in lotus leaves.

The Maramas Family Members

Ruth Cromwell's Family
> Husband: George Cromwell
> Son: John Cromwell married to Becky
> Son: Tom Cromwell
> Brother: Matthew married to Judy
> Mum: Audrey

Cathy Skidmore's Family
> Husband: Dan Skidmore
> Sister: Jackie married to Stephen
> Niece and Nephew: Rosie and Billy
> Parents: Doreen and Barry
> Stepson and Stepdaughter: Mark and Lucy

Stella Benchley-Smythe's Family
> Husband: Peter Benchley-Smythe
> Son: Marcus Benchley-Smythe and partner
> Sebastian

Tam Sui Ling's Family
> Husband: Chan Yuk Kim (YK)
> Son: Michael Chan Li Qiang married to Xiu Ying
> Grandson: Harry Chan Li Wei
> Daughter: Dr. Candy Chan Li Na
> Brother-in-law: Edwin Chan Edwin married to
> Margie

Penny McKenzie's Family
> Husband: Gregory McKenzie
> Twin sons: Felix and Jonathan
> Dogs: Bailey and Toby
> Cats: Suky and Jenny

A Word from the Authors

Thank you for reading our book. As new authors we are eager for reviews, so if you enjoyed this novel, we would really appreciate a few words from you recommending the book to others on Amazon.

Thank you also for journeying with us and the Mahjong Maramas. If you would like to continue this journey and receive news of their upcoming adventure: 'The Mahjong Maramas and the Three Philosophers', please add yourself to our mailing list.

To do this, simply enter your email address on the home page of our website at https://jamiejlaine.com/

Here are a few more links that might interest you:

Meet the Authors: https://jamiejlaine.com/authors
Contact the Authors: https://jamiejlaine.com/contact
Author's Blog Page: https://jamiejlaine.com/blog
Facebook Page: https://www.facebook.com/JamieJLaine

Printed in Great Britain
by Amazon

64576346R00144